DR. HORRIBLE™

AND OTHER HORRIBLE STORIES

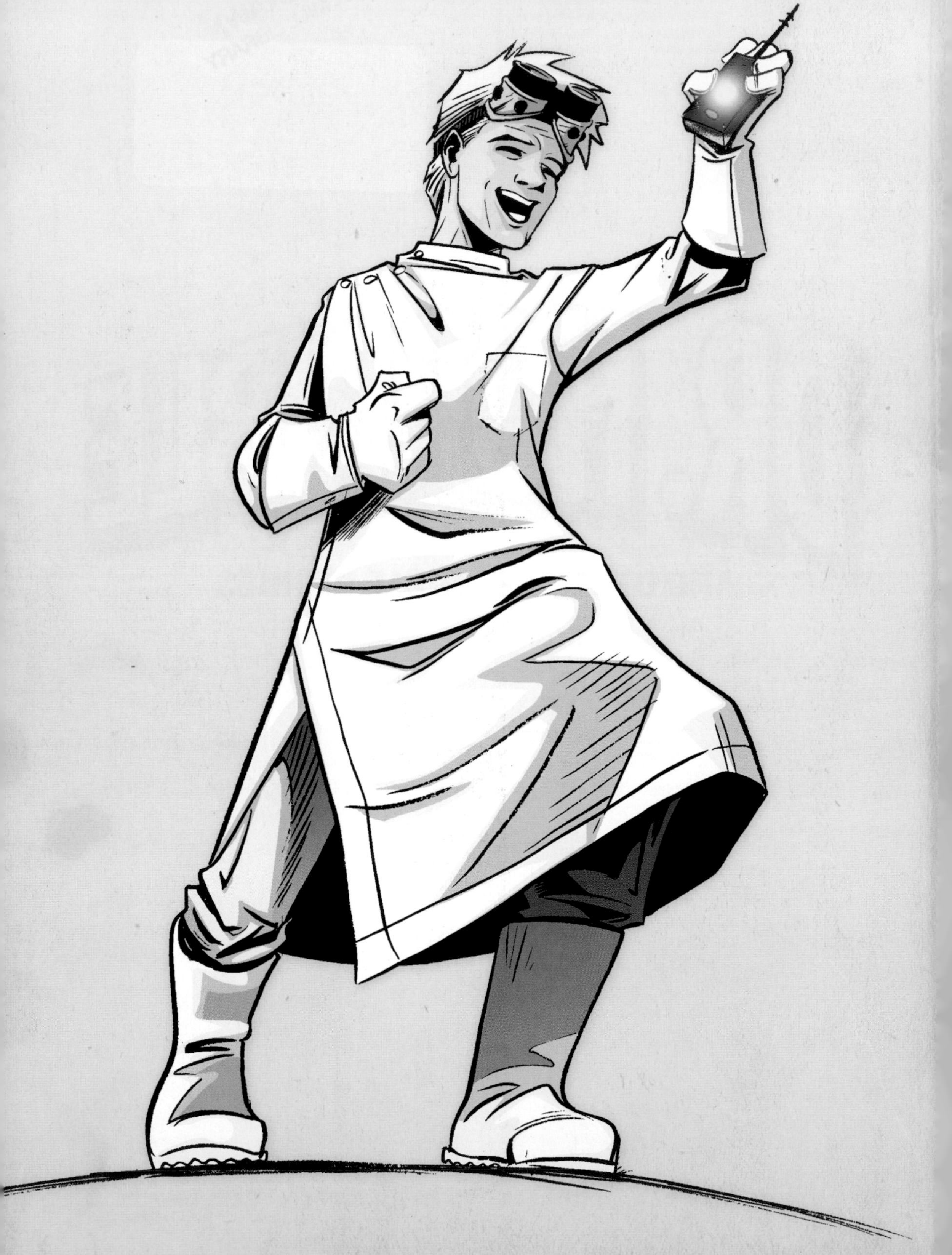

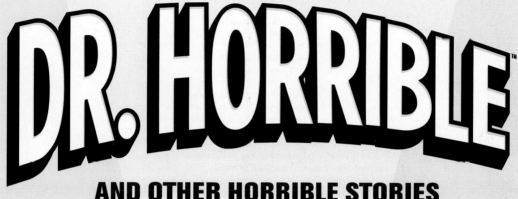

DR. HORRIBLE™

AND OTHER HORRIBLE STORIES

Stories by
ZACK WHEDON

Art by
ERIC CANETE
FAREL DALRYMPLE
JIM RUGG
JOËLLE JONES
SCOTT HEPBURN

Cover art by
KRISTIAN DONALDSON

DARK HORSE BOOKS®

President and Publisher
MIKE RICHARDSON

Editor
SIERRA HAHN

Assistant Editor
DANIEL CHABON

Collection Designer
JOSH ELLIOTT

Special thanks to Joss Whedon, Jed Whedon,
Maurissa Tancharoen, and Scott Allie.

This volume collects the *Dr. Horrible* one-shot; three digital comics from
MySpace Dark Horse Presents ("Captain Hammer: Be Like Me!" "Moist:
Humidity Rising," and "Penny: Keep Your Head Up"), and a new story, "The
Evil League of Evil."

Published by Dark Horse Books
A division of Dark Horse Comics, Inc.
10956 SE Main Street
Milwaukie, OR 97222

darkhorse.com
drhorrible.com

To find a comics shop in your area, call the Comic Shop Locator Service
toll-free at (888) 266-4226.

First edition: September 2010
ISBN 978-1-59582-577-3

1 3 5 7 9 10 8 6 4 2

Printed at 1010 Printing International, Ltd., Guangdong Province, China

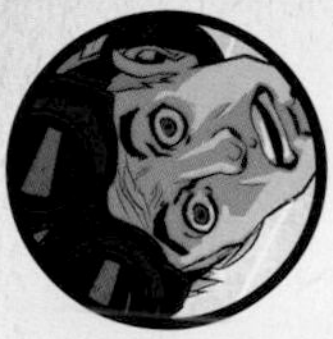

DR. HORRIBLE AND OTHER HORRIBLE STORIES

THE INTRODUCTION

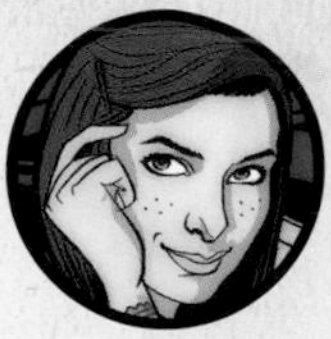

by **Maurissa Tancharoen**, **Jed Whedon**, and **Joss Whedon**, with **special guest**

Just got an e-mail from Dark Horse reminding us to write that intro for the *Dr. Horrible* comics that Zack wrote. Totally forgot about that. Any ideas?
–Maurissa

Truthfully, though they asked all three of us, they probably want Joss to write this thing. Am I right or am I right?
Good luck, Bro!
–Jed

I think they're gonna want the feminine perspective. Maurissa, can you see if Jed will do it?
–Joss

Ha ha ha. Very funny. As I type this it looks sarcastic, but I actually thought that was quite humorous. Just the kind of sprightly wit needed for an intro.
–Jed

I think we should focus on Zack. How he sold out for the big comic-book money. How he turned his back on our little Hollywood artists collective and now he's "gone Portland" and won't return our calls.
Then we should call him a dick. But it should be Mo that does it. It'll sound real coming from Mo. I wouldn't say something like that.
And then maybe we should bring up the content or something? Like what the books are about. Are they about something? I haven't checked.
–Joss

You know I'm always down to call Zack a dick. That's easy. Can that be my one and only contribution to this whole intro thing? 'Cause the thought of doing anything beyond that is giving me a headache.
I guess we could talk about how awesome and supportive the fans are. Or how cool it is to see the world of *Dr. Horrible* fleshed out in this format? Or talk about Zack's ever-growing beard. Seems like he's going for a homeless vibe lately, right? Ooh! We could link Zack's homeless vibe with all the homeless stuff in *Dr. H.* Check me out, breaking out a theme for this intro!
Anyway, Zack is a dick.
XOXO.
–Maurissa

This whole direction might be wrong. Zack is SUPER sensitive. Like weirdly sensitive. We should say nice things maybe instead. I mean, we'd have to make them up, but it would be good for his self-esteem. He needs that 'cause he's not very attractive.
–Jed

Zack is very punctual?
Zack has a good handshake?
I got nothing.
–Joss

Ooooh, maybe we can pawn it off on the actors. No applause, please.
–Maurissa

Good idea! Mo comes through in the clutch. What about Felicia?
–Joss

She's too busy.
–Maurissa

Neil?
–Jed

He's too famous.
–Maurissa

Nathan?
–Joss

He's just right. Joss, why don't you send him an e-mail right now…
–Maurissa

Nathan,
Would you be willing to write an intro for the *Dr. Horrible* comic-book series? Doesn't have to be big, just, you know, complimentary. How the writing and the art are brilliant, etc. That would be great. Thanks in advance!
–Joss

Unsubscribe.
–Nathan
Sent from my iPhone

CAPTAIN HAMMER: BE LIKE ME!

Story by
ZACK WHEDON

Pencils by
ERIC CANETE

Colors by
DAVE STEWART

Letters by
NATE PIEKOS OF BLAMBOT®

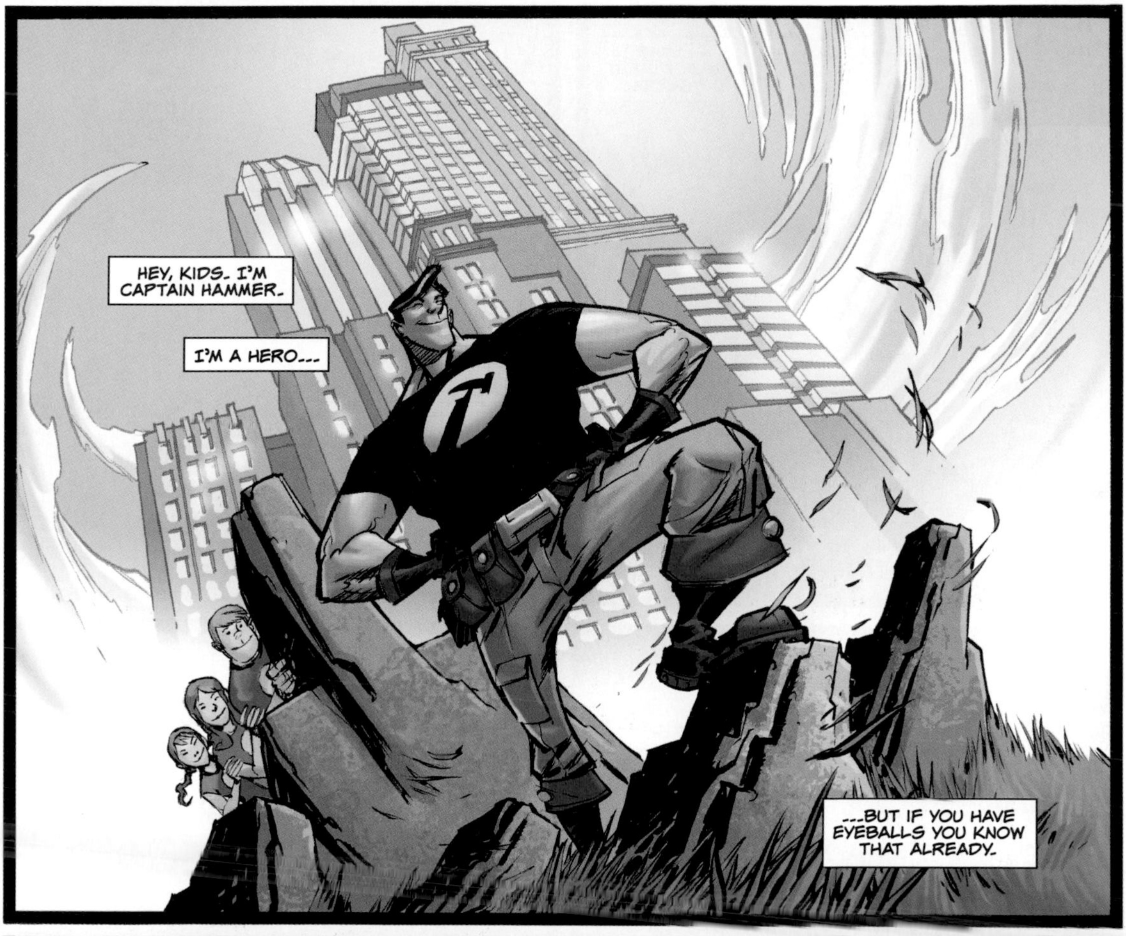
HEY, KIDS. I'M CAPTAIN HAMMER.
I'M A HERO...
...BUT IF YOU HAVE EYEBALLS YOU KNOW THAT ALREADY.

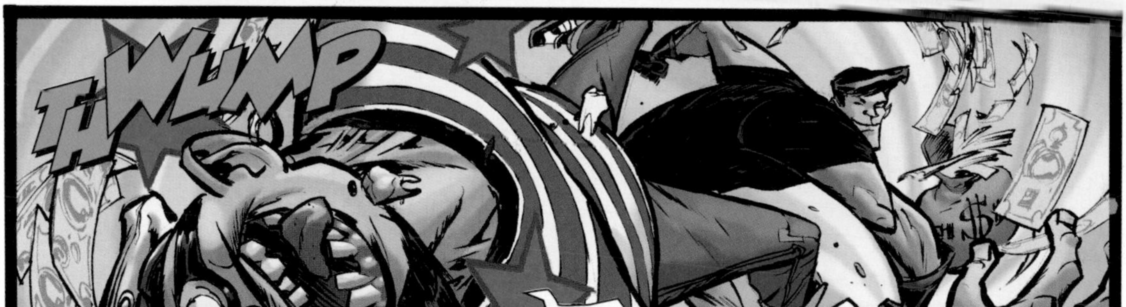
THWUMP
GUH
I MAY MAKE THIS LOOK EASY, BUT IT'S HARD WORK.

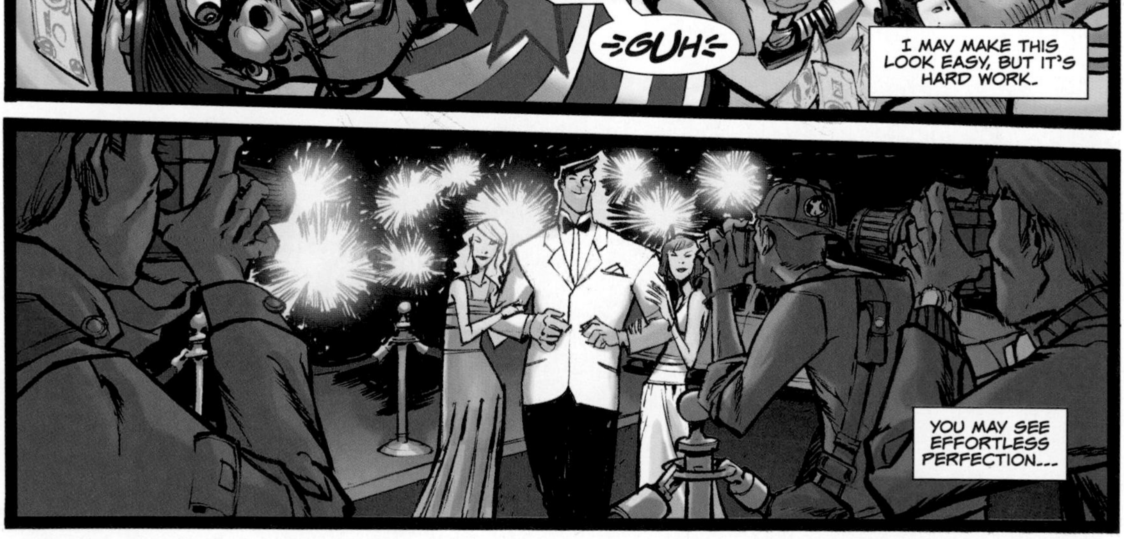
YOU MAY SEE EFFORTLESS PERFECTION...

...THE EMBODIMENT OF GOOD...

THANK YOU!

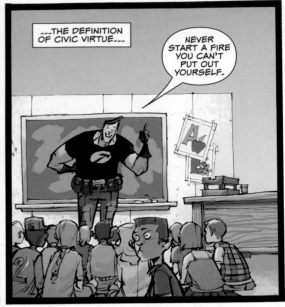

...THE DEFINITION OF CIVIC VIRTUE...

NEVER START A FIRE YOU CAN'T PUT OUT YOURSELF.

...BUT I WASN'T BORN WITH IT...

CRACK

...I WAS BORN WITH A FULL HEAD OF HAIR AND THE ABILITY TO BENCH PRESS FIVE HUNDRED POUNDS...

CAPTAIN HAMMER

...BUT TO BE A HERO YOU NEED HARD-EARNED SKILLS.

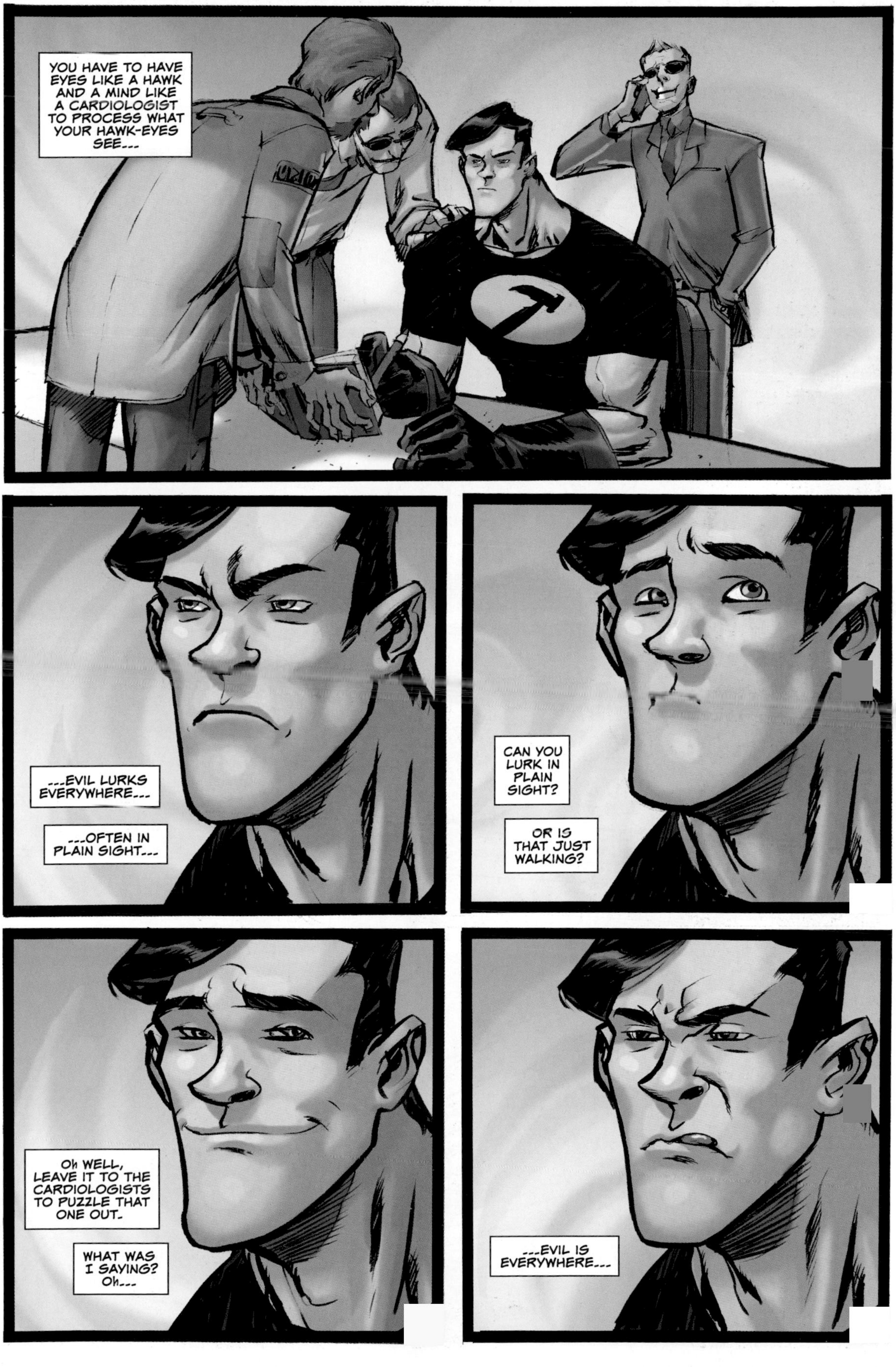
YOU HAVE TO HAVE EYES LIKE A HAWK AND A MIND LIKE A CARDIOLOGIST TO PROCESS WHAT YOUR HAWK-EYES SEE---
---EVIL LURKS EVERYWHERE---
---OFTEN IN PLAIN SIGHT---
CAN YOU LURK IN PLAIN SIGHT?
OR IS THAT JUST WALKING?
Oh WELL, LEAVE IT TO THE CARDIOLOGISTS TO PUZZLE THAT ONE OUT.
WHAT WAS I SAYING? Oh---
---EVIL IS EVERYWHERE---

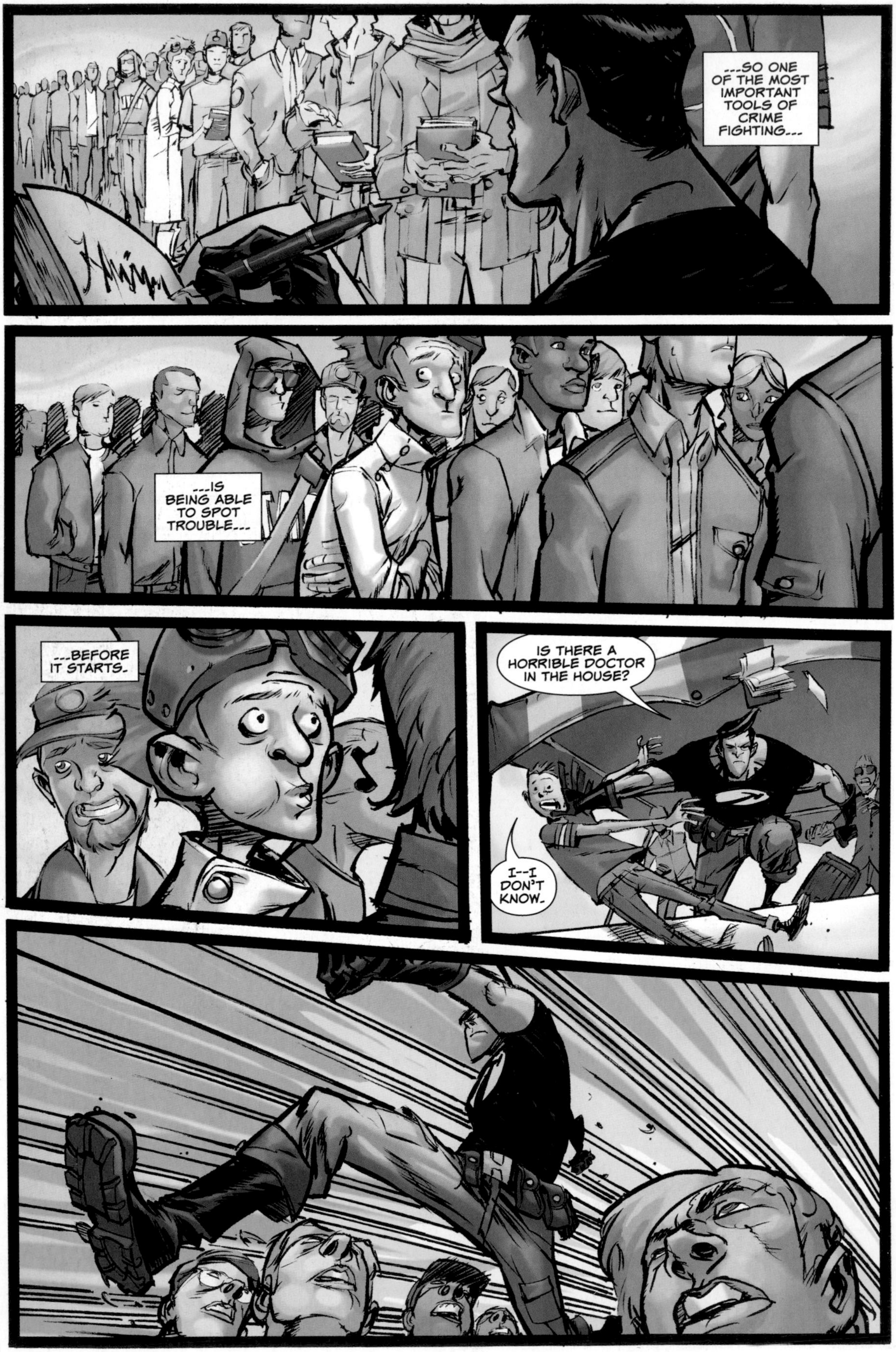
...SO ONE OF THE MOST IMPORTANT TOOLS OF CRIME FIGHTING...
...IS BEING ABLE TO SPOT TROUBLE...
...BEFORE IT STARTS.
IS THERE A HORRIBLE DOCTOR IN THE HOUSE?
I--I DON'T KNOW.

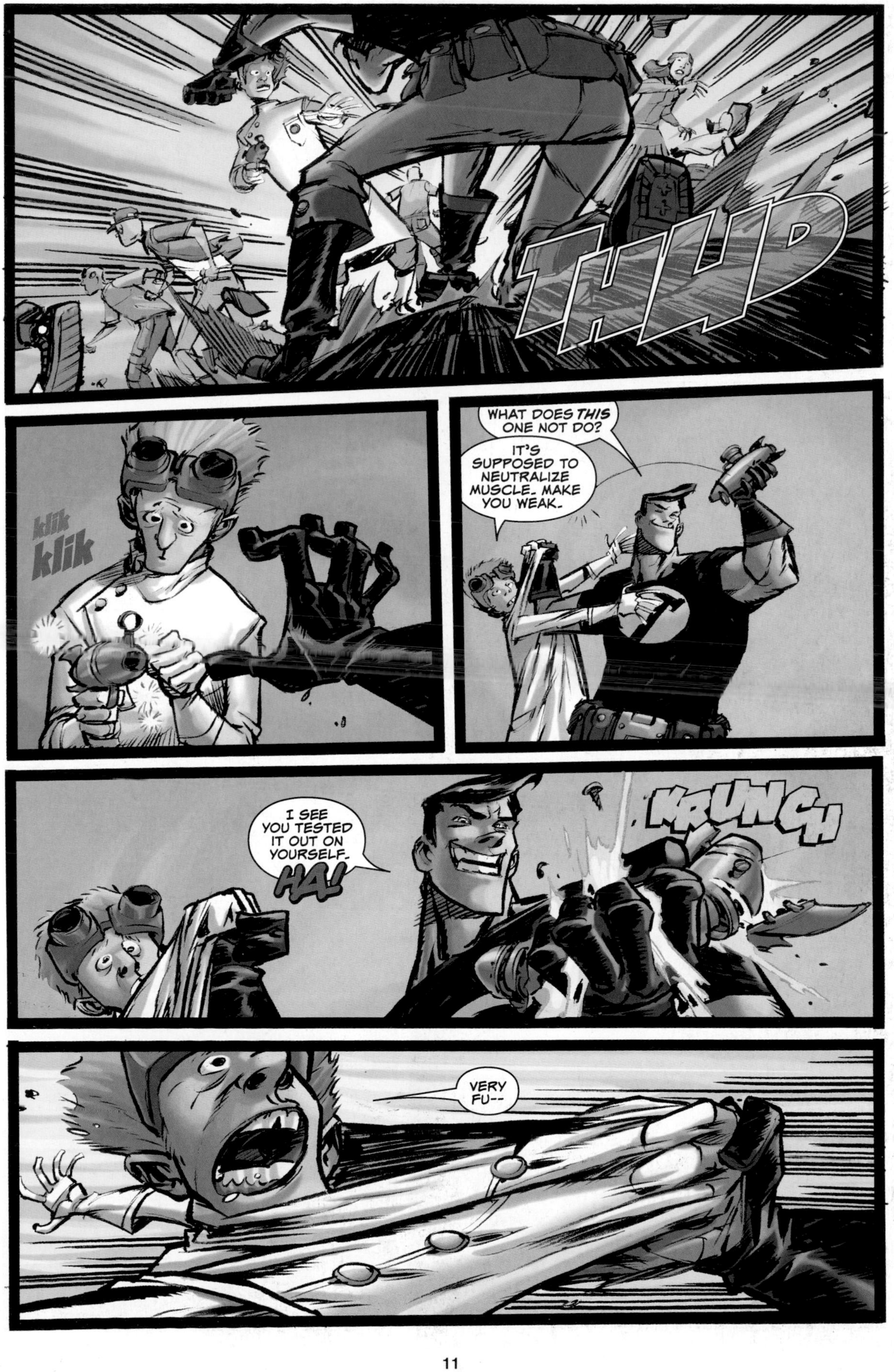
THUD
klik
klik
WHAT DOES THIS ONE NOT DO?
IT'S SUPPOSED TO NEUTRALIZE MUSCLE. MAKE YOU WEAK.
I SEE YOU TESTED IT OUT ON YOURSELF.
HA!
KRUNCH
VERY FU--

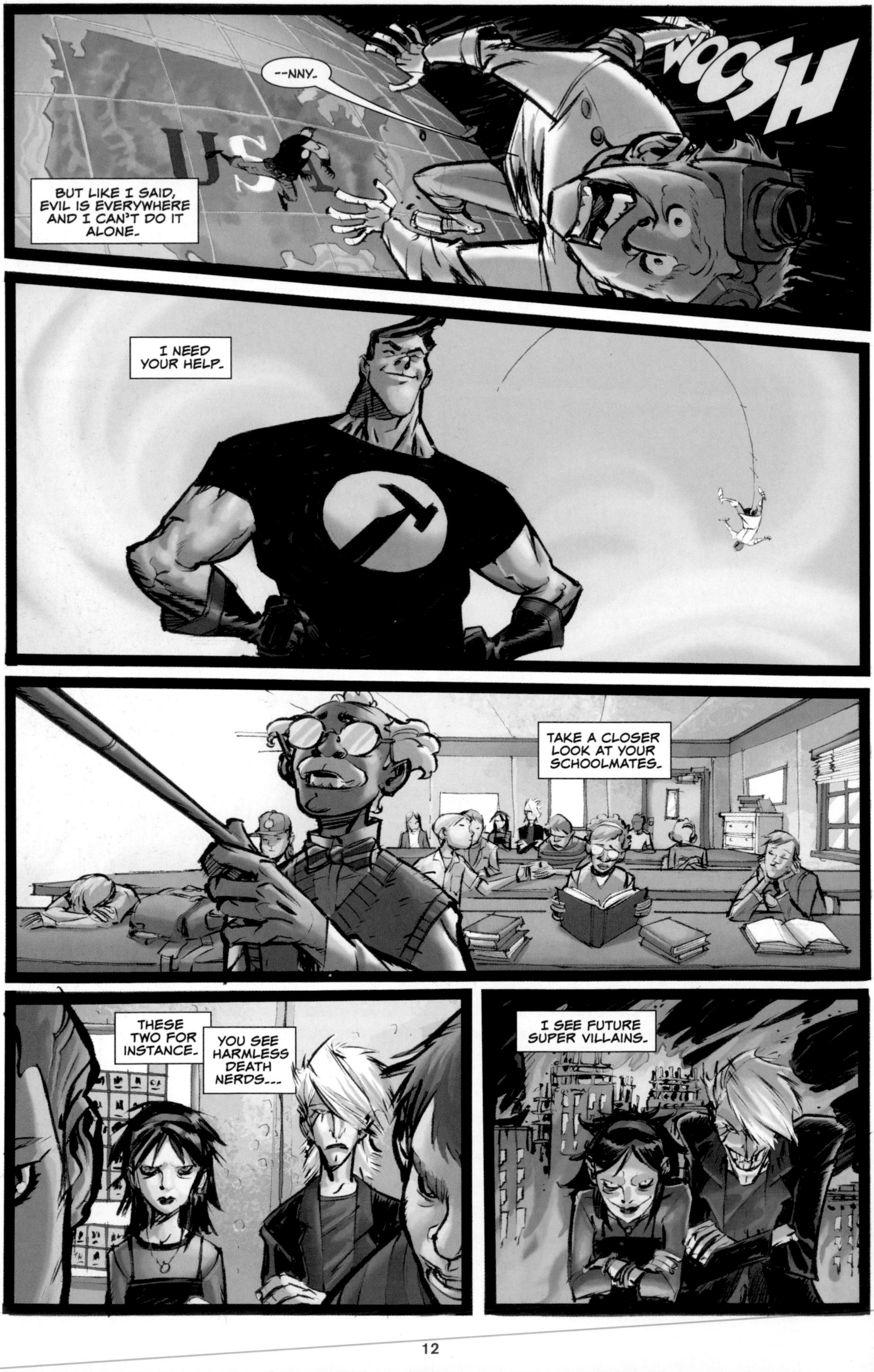
--NNY.
WOOSH
BUT LIKE I SAID, EVIL IS EVERYWHERE AND I CAN'T DO IT ALONE.
I NEED YOUR HELP.
TAKE A CLOSER LOOK AT YOUR SCHOOLMATES.
THESE TWO FOR INSTANCE.
YOU SEE HARMLESS DEATH NERDS...
I SEE FUTURE SUPER VILLAINS.

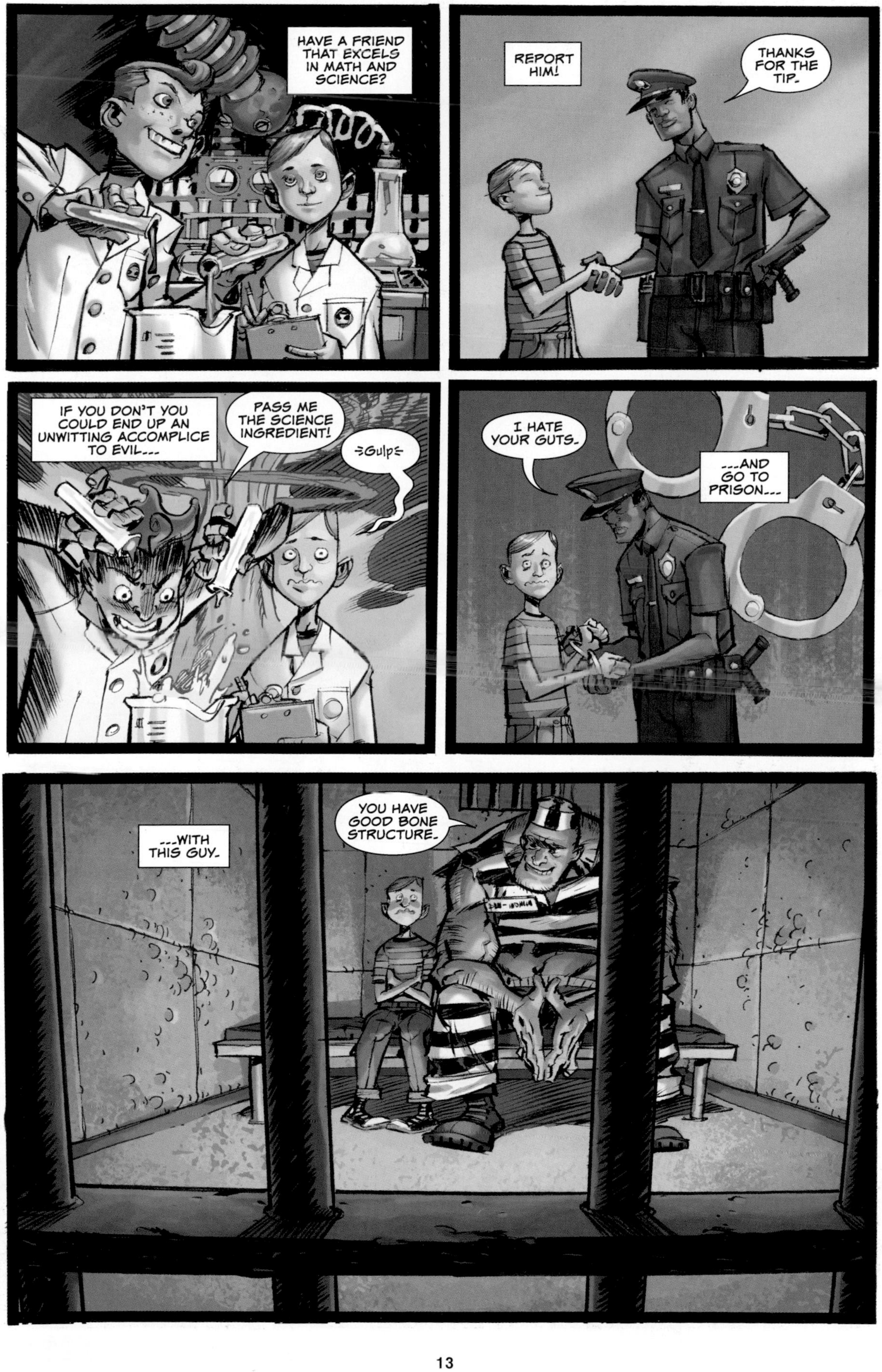
HAVE A FRIEND THAT EXCELS IN MATH AND SCIENCE?
REPORT HIM!
THANKS FOR THE TIP.
IF YOU DON'T YOU COULD END UP AN UNWITTING ACCOMPLICE TO EVIL...
PASS ME THE SCIENCE INGREDIENT!
Gulp
I HATE YOUR GUTS.
...AND GO TO PRISON...
...WITH THIS GUY.
YOU HAVE GOOD BONE STRUCTURE.

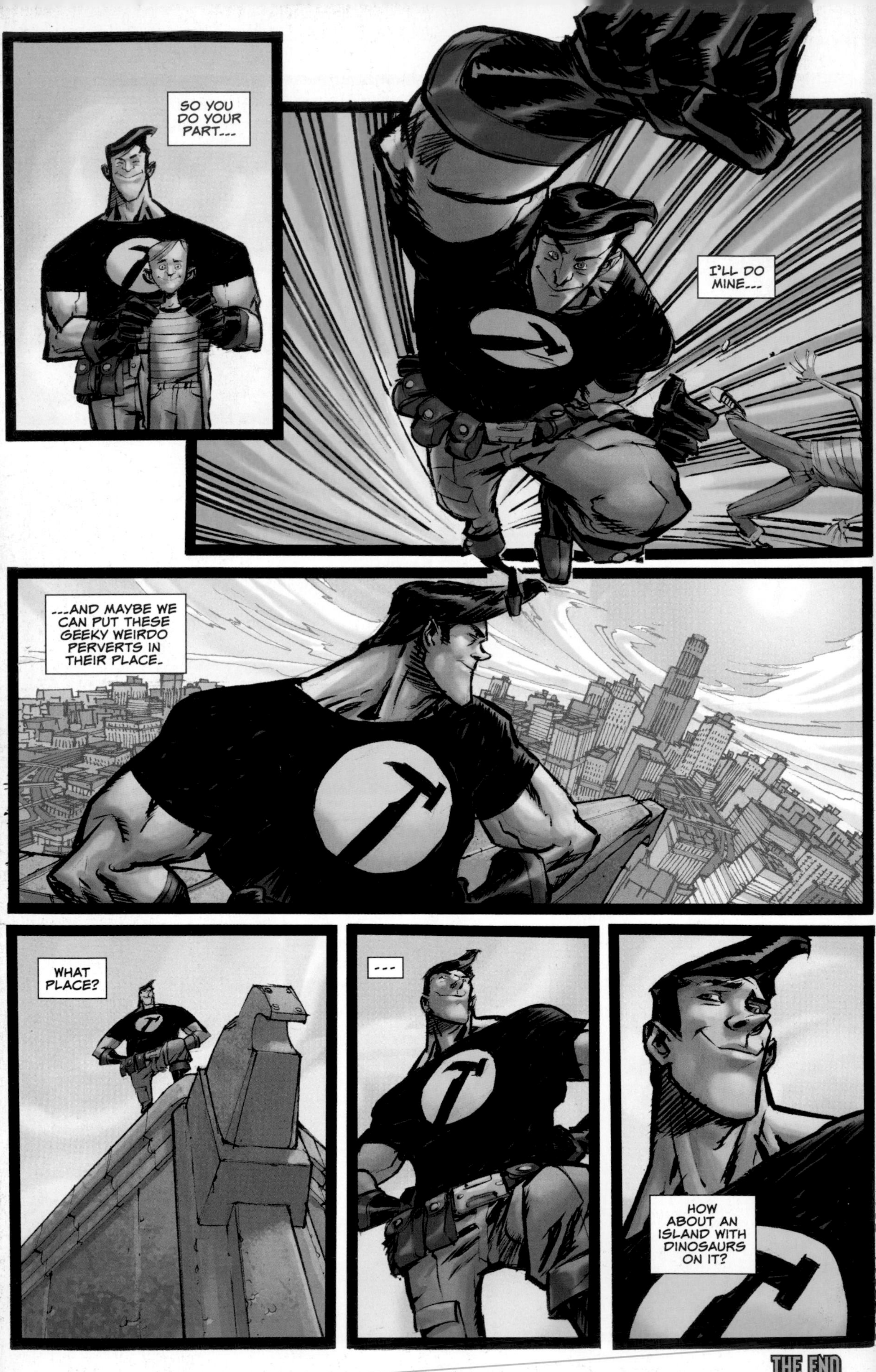
SO YOU DO YOUR PART...
I'LL DO MINE...
...AND MAYBE WE CAN PUT THESE GEEKY WEIRDO PERVERTS IN THEIR PLACE.
WHAT PLACE?
...
HOW ABOUT AN ISLAND WITH DINOSAURS ON IT?
THE END

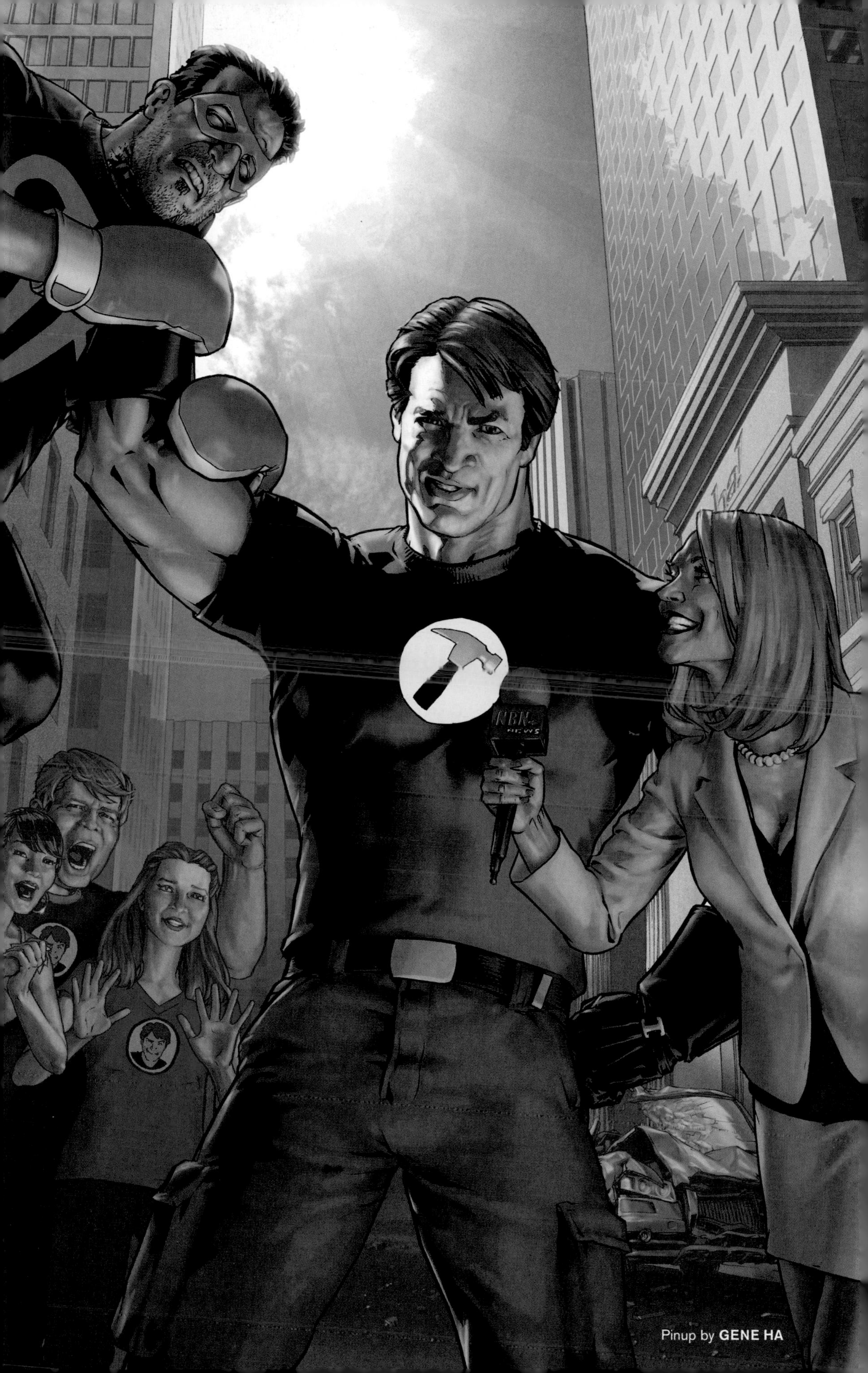

Pinup by **GENE HA**

MOIST: HUMIDITY RISING

Story by
ZACK WHEDON

Art by
FAREL DALRYMPLE

Colors by
DAN JACKSON

Letters by
NATE PIEKOS OF BLAMBOT®

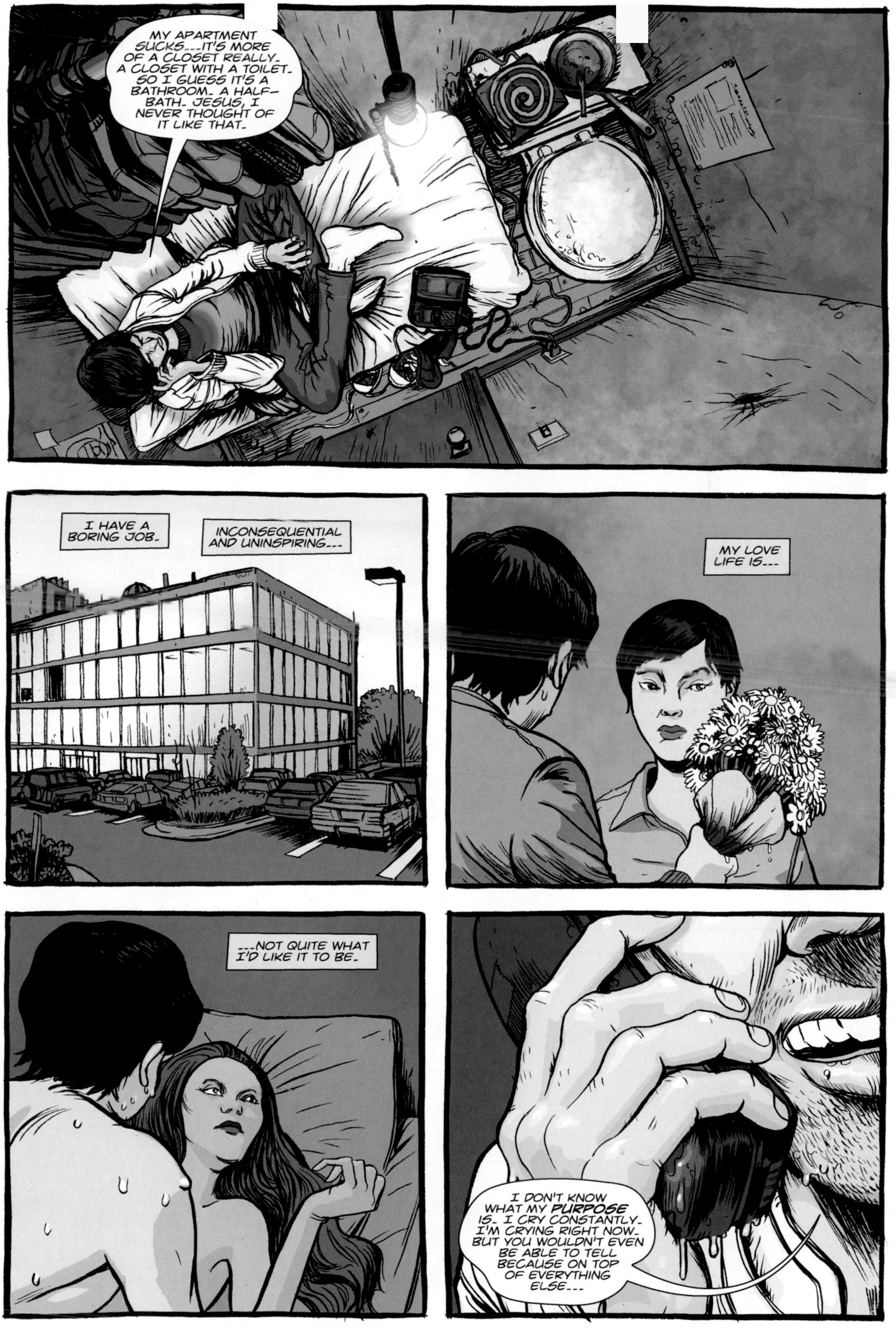

MY APARTMENT SUCKS...IT'S MORE OF A CLOSET REALLY. A CLOSET WITH A TOILET. SO I GUESS IT'S A BATHROOM. A HALF-BATH. JESUS, I NEVER THOUGHT OF IT LIKE THAT.
I HAVE A BORING JOB.
INCONSEQUENTIAL AND UNINSPIRING...
MY LOVE LIFE IS...
...NOT QUITE WHAT I'D LIKE IT TO BE.
I DON'T KNOW WHAT MY PURPOSE IS. I CRY CONSTANTLY. I'M CRYING RIGHT NOW. BUT YOU WOULDN'T EVEN BE ABLE TO TELL BECAUSE ON TOP OF EVERYTHING ELSE...

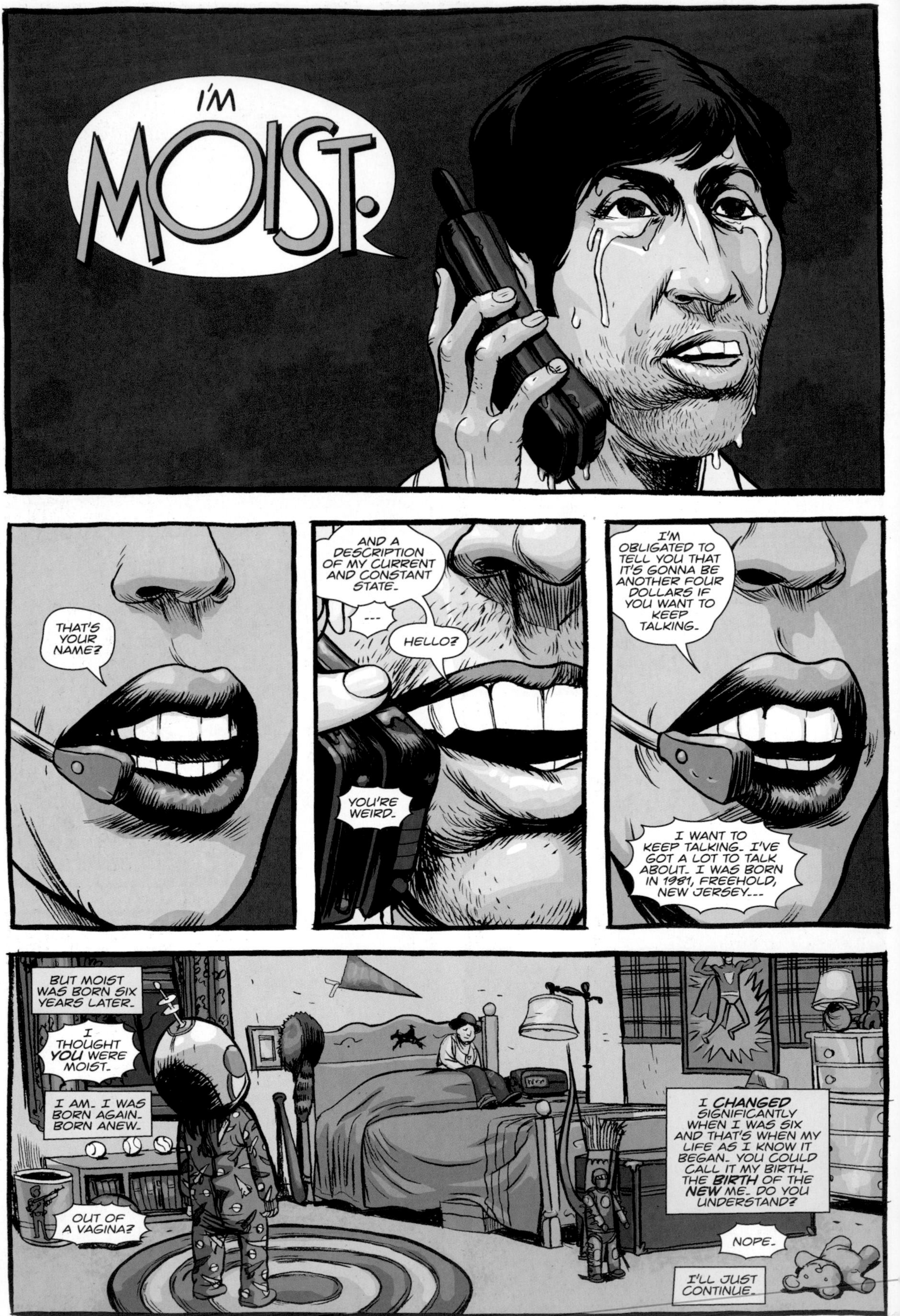
I'M MOIST.
THAT'S YOUR NAME?
AND A DESCRIPTION OF MY CURRENT AND CONSTANT STATE.
...
HELLO?
YOU'RE WEIRD.
I'M OBLIGATED TO TELL YOU THAT IT'S GONNA BE ANOTHER FOUR DOLLARS IF YOU WANT TO KEEP TALKING.
I WANT TO KEEP TALKING. I'VE GOT A LOT TO TALK ABOUT. I WAS BORN IN 1981, FREEHOLD, NEW JERSEY...
BUT MOIST WAS BORN SIX YEARS LATER.
I THOUGHT YOU WERE MOIST.
I AM. I WAS BORN AGAIN. BORN ANEW.
OUT OF A VAGINA?
I CHANGED SIGNIFICANTLY WHEN I WAS SIX AND THAT'S WHEN MY LIFE AS I KNOW IT BEGAN. YOU COULD CALL IT MY BIRTH. THE BIRTH OF THE NEW ME. DO YOU UNDERSTAND?
NOPE.
I'LL JUST CONTINUE.

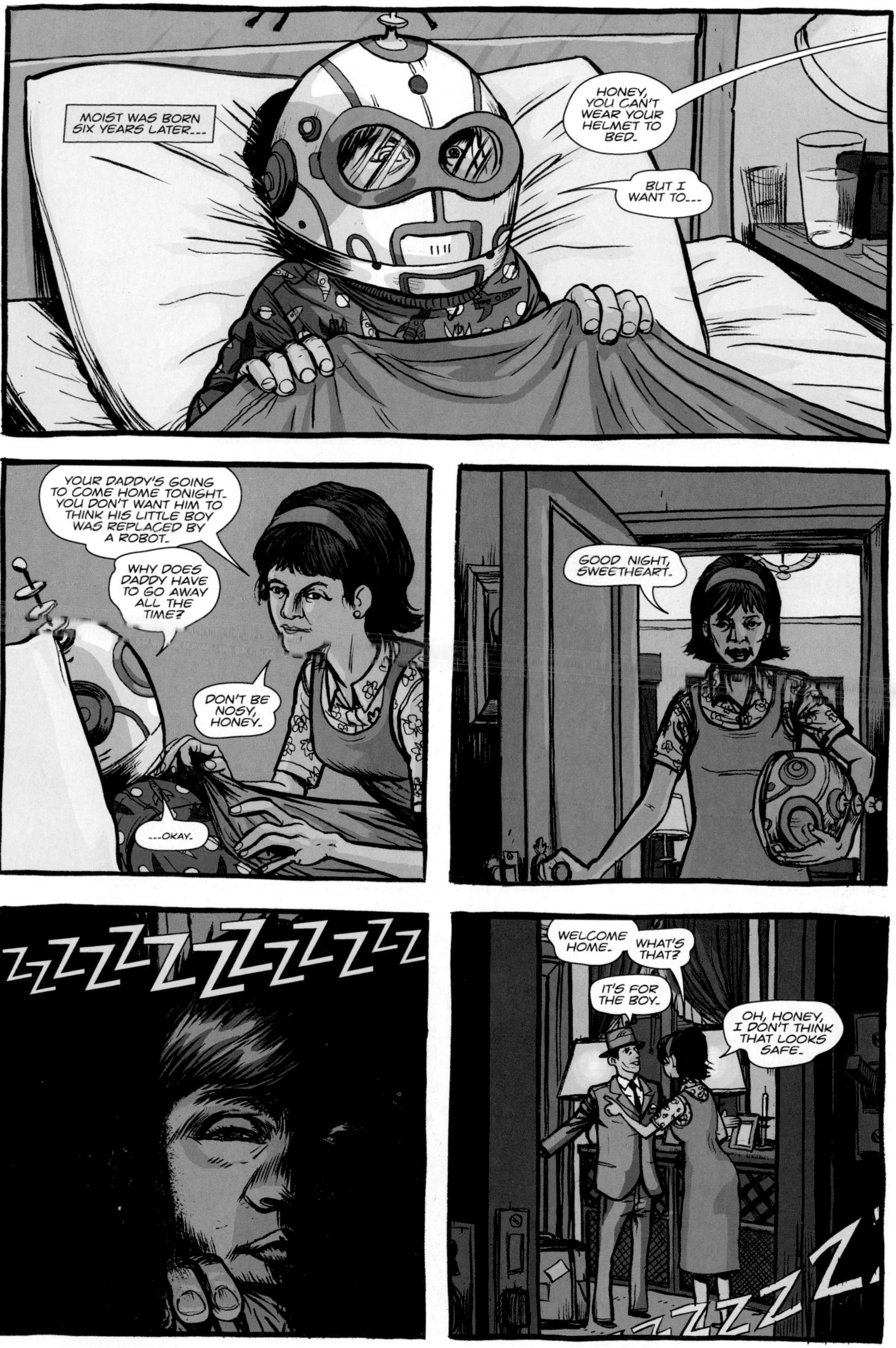
MOIST WAS BORN SIX YEARS LATER...
HONEY, YOU CAN'T WEAR YOUR HELMET TO BED.
BUT I WANT TO...
YOUR DADDY'S GOING TO COME HOME TONIGHT. YOU DON'T WANT HIM TO THINK HIS LITTLE BOY WAS REPLACED BY A ROBOT.
WHY DOES DADDY HAVE TO GO AWAY ALL THE TIME?
DON'T BE NOSY, HONEY.
...OKAY.
GOOD NIGHT, SWEETHEART.
ZZZZZZZZZZZZZZZ
WELCOME HOME.
WHAT'S THAT?
IT'S FOR THE BOY.
OH, HONEY, I DON'T THINK THAT LOOKS SAFE.
ZZZZZZZ

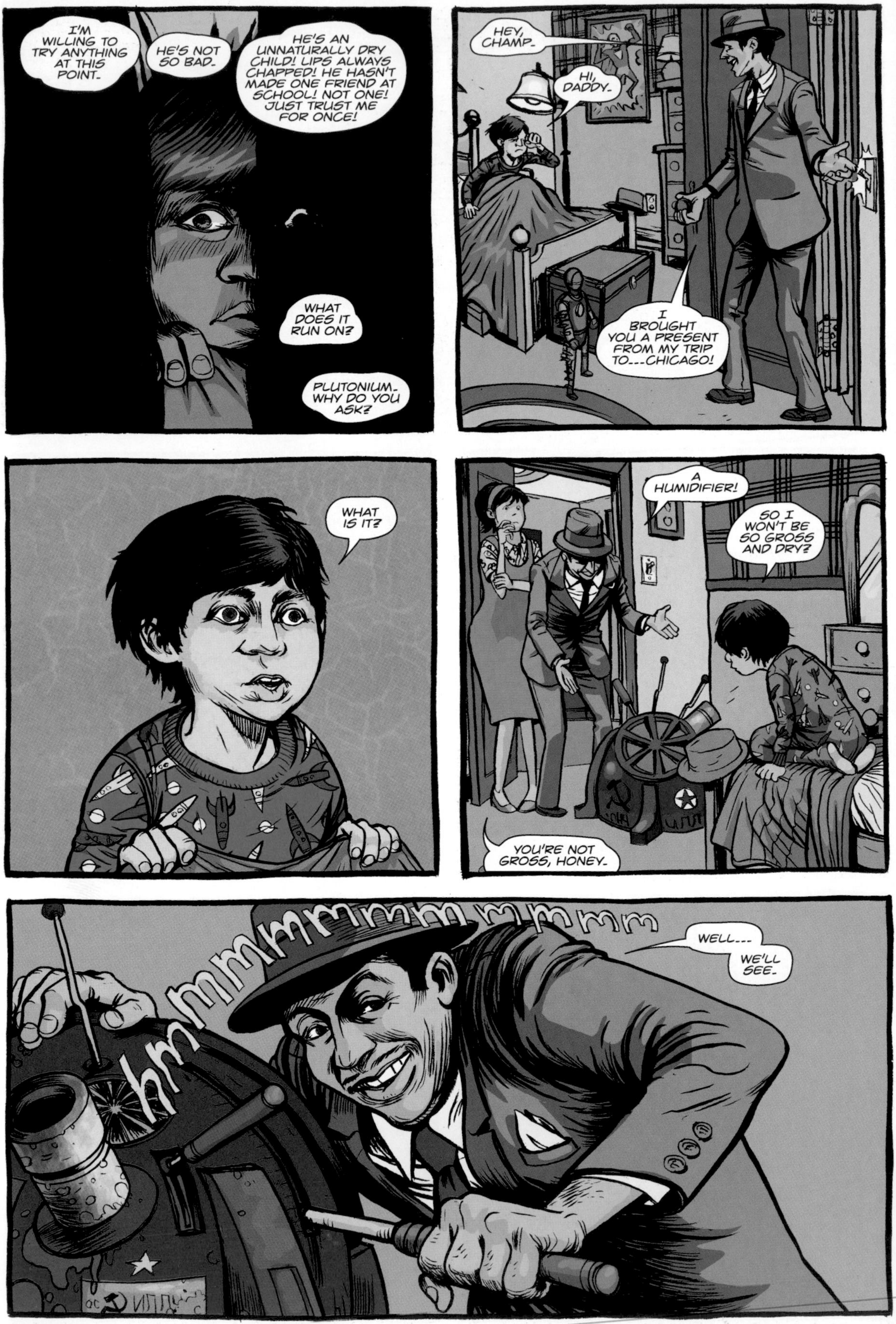
I'M WILLING TO TRY ANYTHING AT THIS POINT.
HE'S NOT SO BAD.
HE'S AN UNNATURALLY DRY CHILD! LIPS ALWAYS CHAPPED! HE HASN'T MADE ONE FRIEND AT SCHOOL! NOT ONE! JUST TRUST ME FOR ONCE!
WHAT DOES IT RUN ON?
PLUTONIUM. WHY DO YOU ASK?
HEY, CHAMP.
HI, DADDY.
I BROUGHT YOU A PRESENT FROM MY TRIP TO...CHICAGO!
WHAT IS IT?
A HUMIDIFIER!
SO I WON'T BE SO GROSS AND DRY?
YOU'RE NOT GROSS, HONEY.
hmmmmmmmmmmmmm
WELL...
WE'LL SEE.

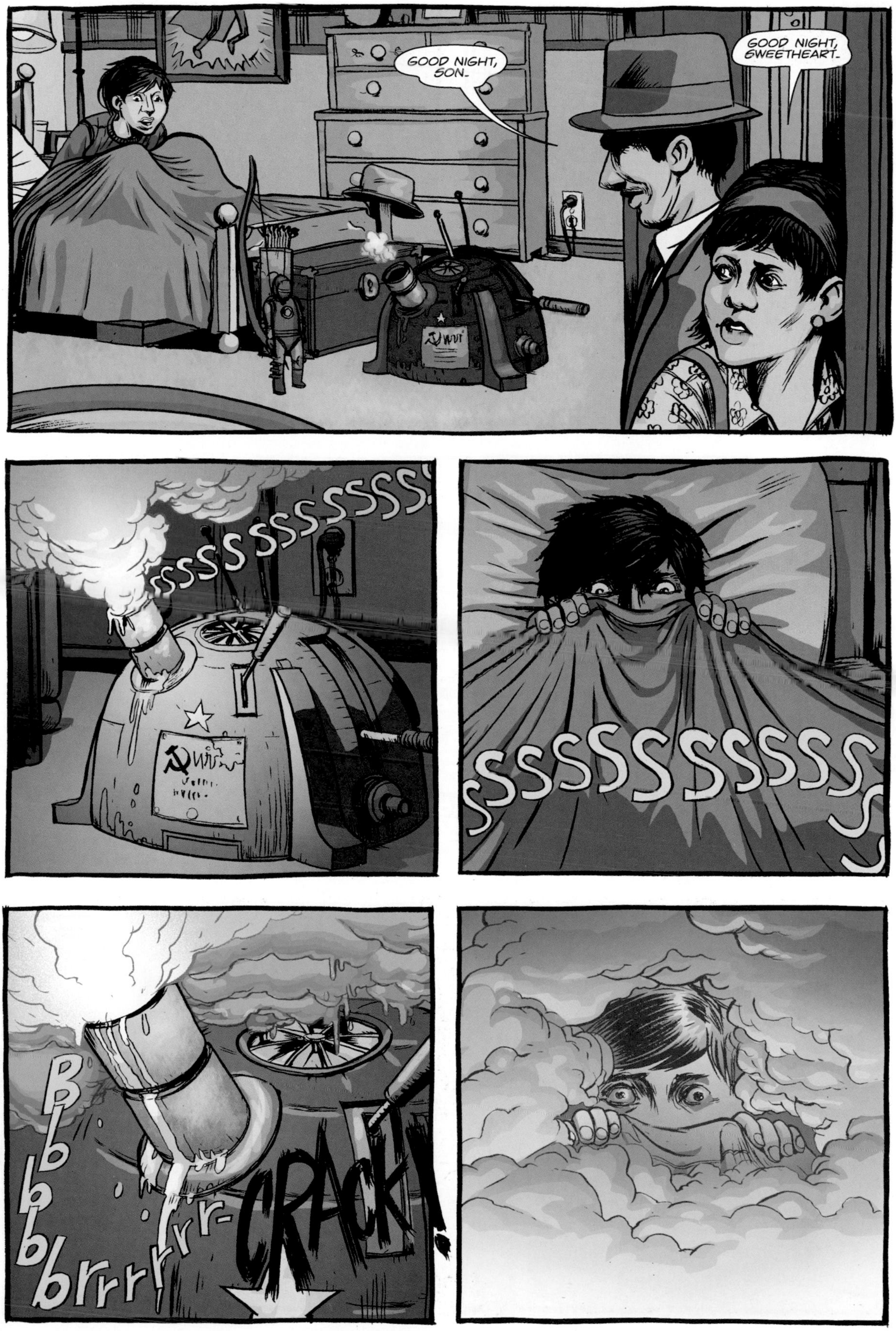
GOOD NIGHT, SON.
GOOD NIGHT, SWEETHEART.
sssSSSSSSSSSSS
SSSSSSSSSSSSS
Bbbbbbrrrrrrr-CRACK!

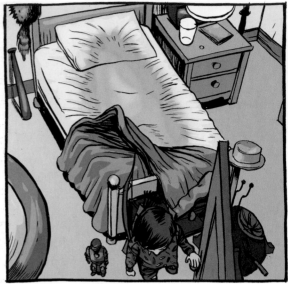

SQUILP

HEY, CHAMP, HOW DID YOU LIKE THAT—

EEEG!

THAT'S HOW IT HAPPENED...

22

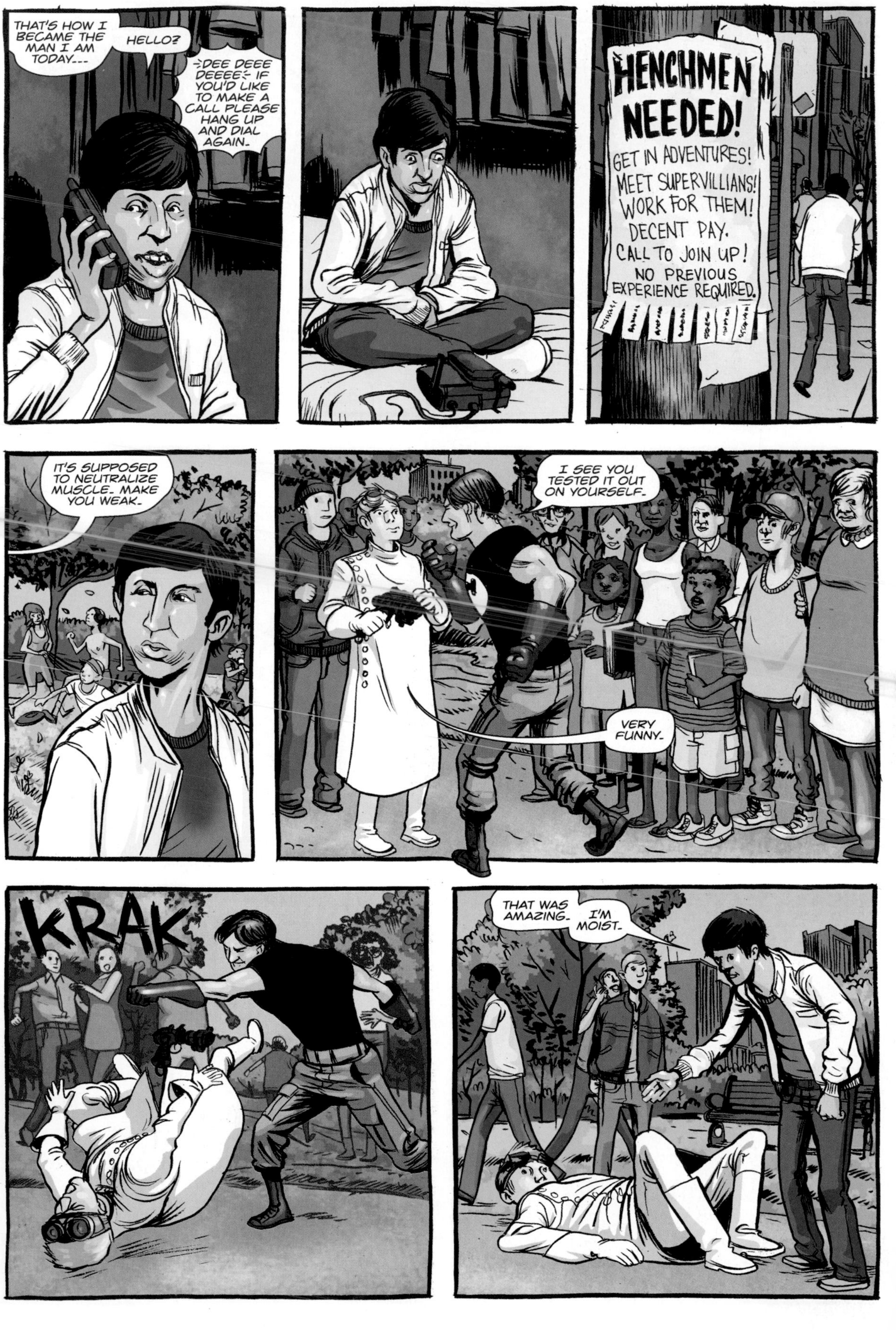
THAT'S HOW I BECAME THE MAN I AM TODAY...
HELLO?
~DEE DEEE DEEEE~ IF YOU'D LIKE TO MAKE A CALL PLEASE HANG UP AND DIAL AGAIN.
HENCHMEN NEEDED!
GET IN ADVENTURES!
MEET SUPERVILLIANS!
WORK FOR THEM!
DECENT PAY.
CALL TO JOIN UP!
NO PREVIOUS EXPERIENCE REQUIRED.
IT'S SUPPOSED TO NEUTRALIZE MUSCLE. MAKE YOU WEAK.
I SEE YOU TESTED IT OUT ON YOURSELF.
VERY FUNNY.
KRAK
THAT WAS AMAZING.
I'M MOIST.

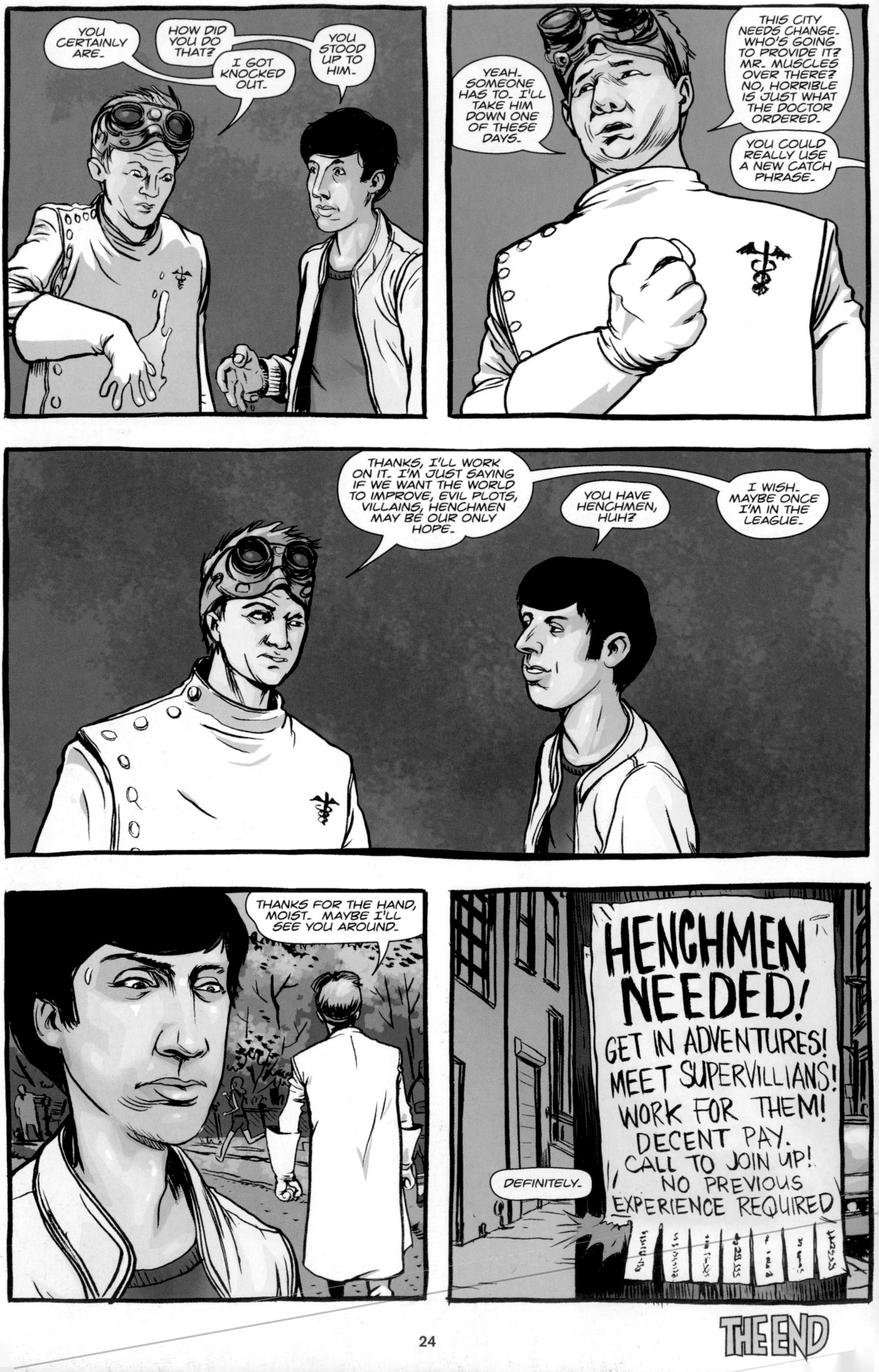

YOU CERTAINLY ARE.
HOW DID YOU DO THAT?
I GOT KNOCKED OUT.
YOU STOOD UP TO HIM.
YEAH. SOMEONE HAS TO. I'LL TAKE HIM DOWN ONE OF THESE DAYS.
THIS CITY NEEDS CHANGE. WHO'S GOING TO PROVIDE IT? MR. MUSCLES OVER THERE? NO, HORRIBLE IS JUST WHAT THE DOCTOR ORDERED.
YOU COULD REALLY USE A NEW CATCH PHRASE.
THANKS, I'LL WORK ON IT. I'M JUST SAYING IF WE WANT THE WORLD TO IMPROVE, EVIL PLOTS, VILLAINS, HENCHMEN MAY BE OUR ONLY HOPE.
YOU HAVE HENCHMEN, HUH?
I WISH. MAYBE ONCE I'M IN THE LEAGUE.
THANKS FOR THE HAND, MOIST. MAYBE I'LL SEE YOU AROUND.
HENCHMEN NEEDED!
GET IN ADVENTURES!
MEET SUPERVILLIANS!
WORK FOR THEM!
DECENT PAY.
CALL TO JOIN UP!
NO PREVIOUS EXPERIENCE REQUIRED
DEFINITELY.
THE END

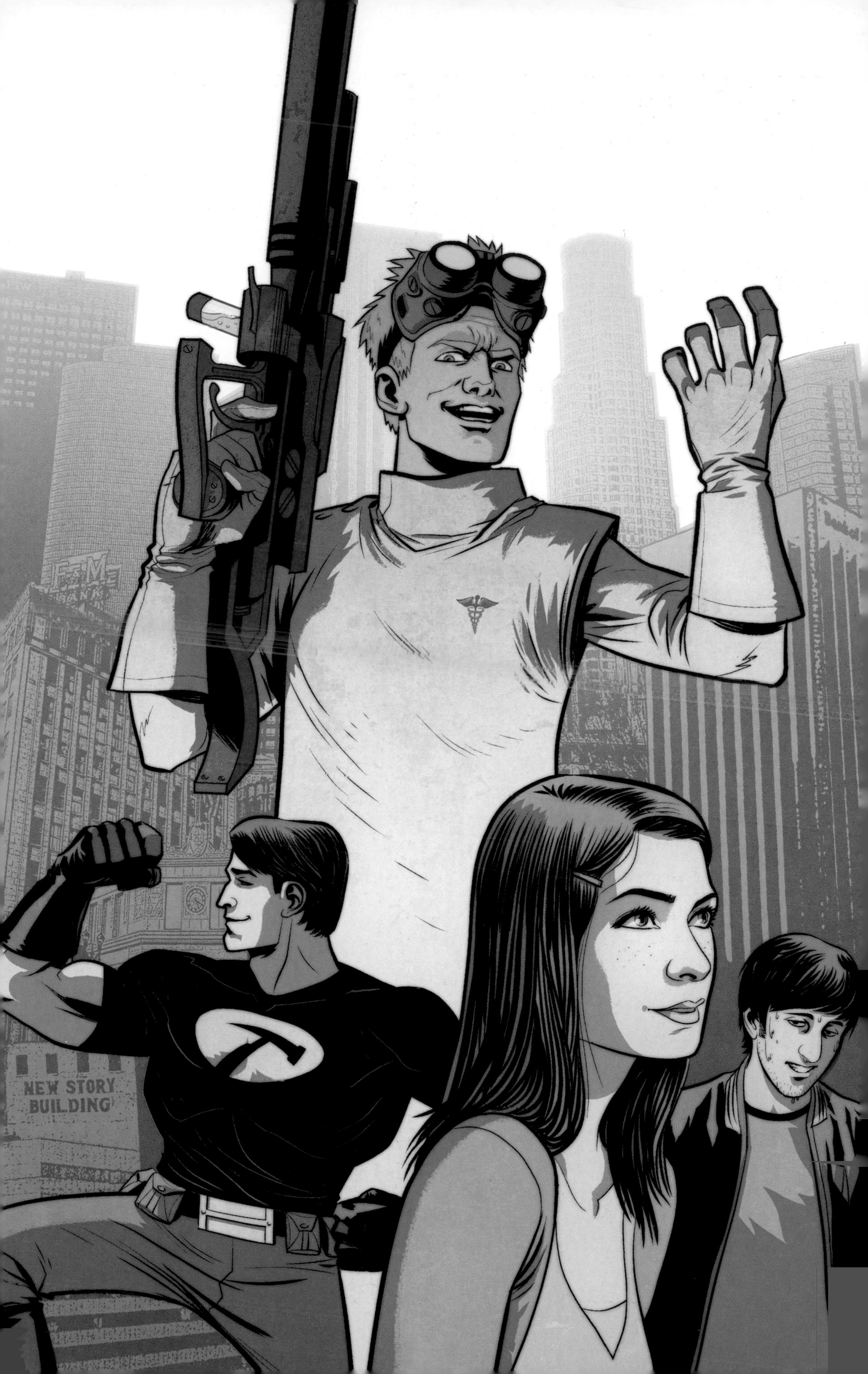

NEW STORY
BUILDING

PENNY: KEEP YOUR HEAD UP

Story by
ZACK WHEDON

Art by
JIM RUGG

Colors by
DAN JACKSON

Letters by
NATE PIEKOS OF BLAMBOT®

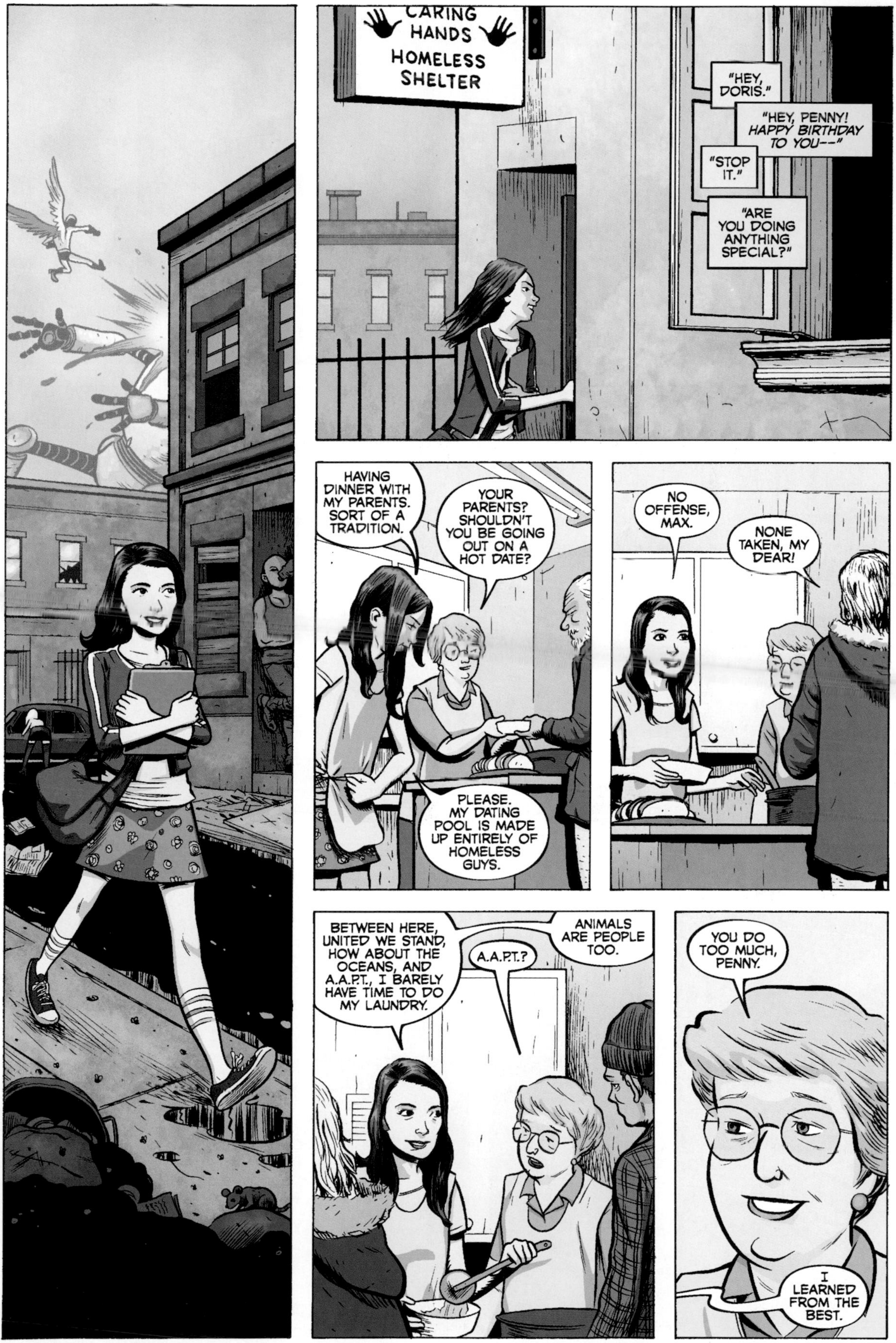
CARING HANDS HOMELESS SHELTER
"HEY, DORIS."
"HEY, PENNY! HAPPY BIRTHDAY TO YOU--"
"STOP IT."
"ARE YOU DOING ANYTHING SPECIAL?"
HAVING DINNER WITH MY PARENTS. SORT OF A TRADITION.
YOUR PARENTS? SHOULDN'T YOU BE GOING OUT ON A HOT DATE?
PLEASE. MY DATING POOL IS MADE UP ENTIRELY OF HOMELESS GUYS.
NO OFFENSE, MAX.
NONE TAKEN, MY DEAR!
BETWEEN HERE, UNITED WE STAND, HOW ABOUT THE OCEANS, AND A.A.P.T., I BARELY HAVE TIME TO DO MY LAUNDRY.
A.A.P.T.?
ANIMALS ARE PEOPLE TOO.
YOU DO TOO MUCH, PENNY.
I LEARNED FROM THE BEST.

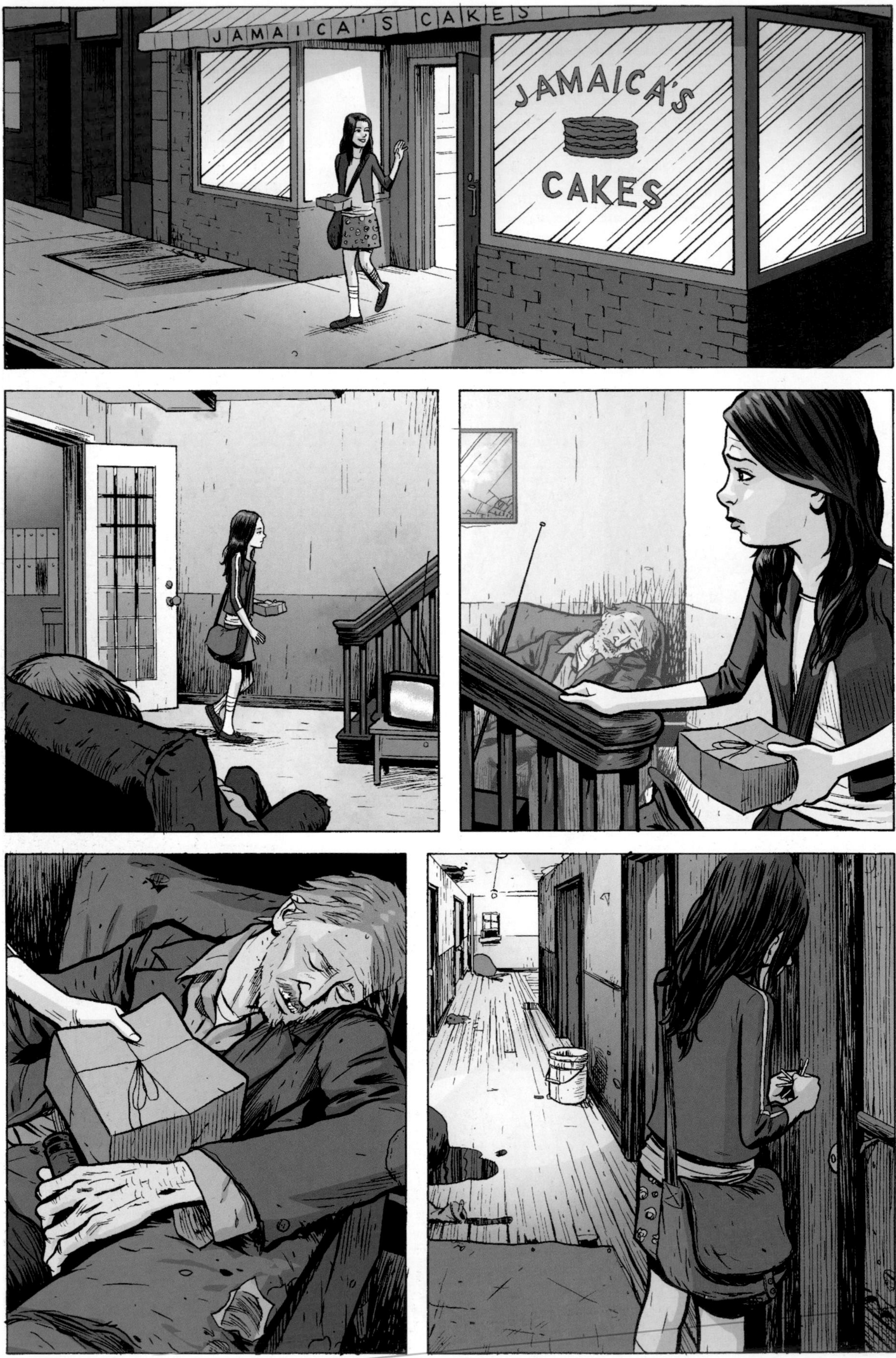

JAMAICA'S CAKES
JAMAICA'S
CAKES

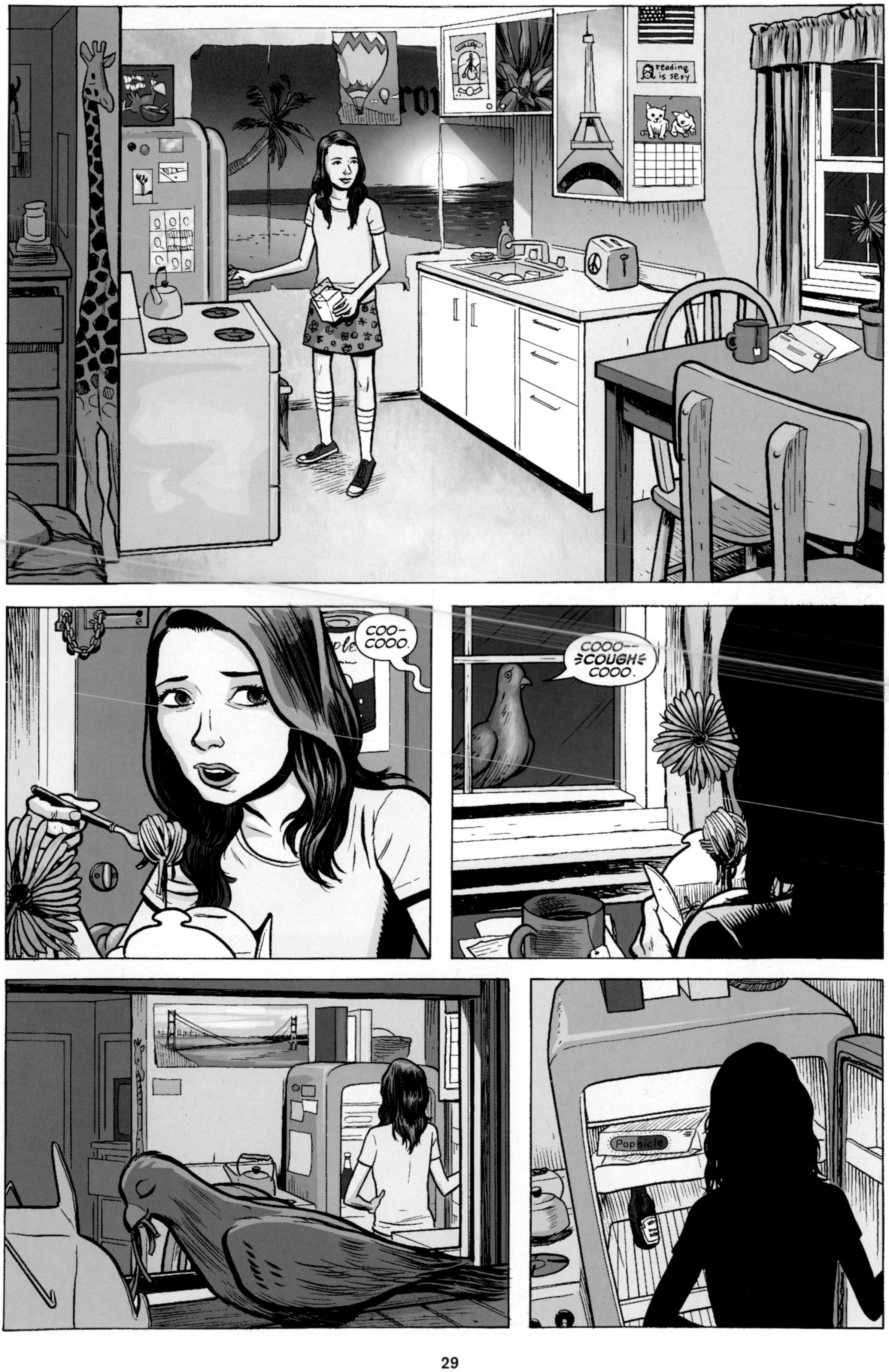
reading is sexy
COO-COOO.
COOO--COUGH COOO.
Popsicle

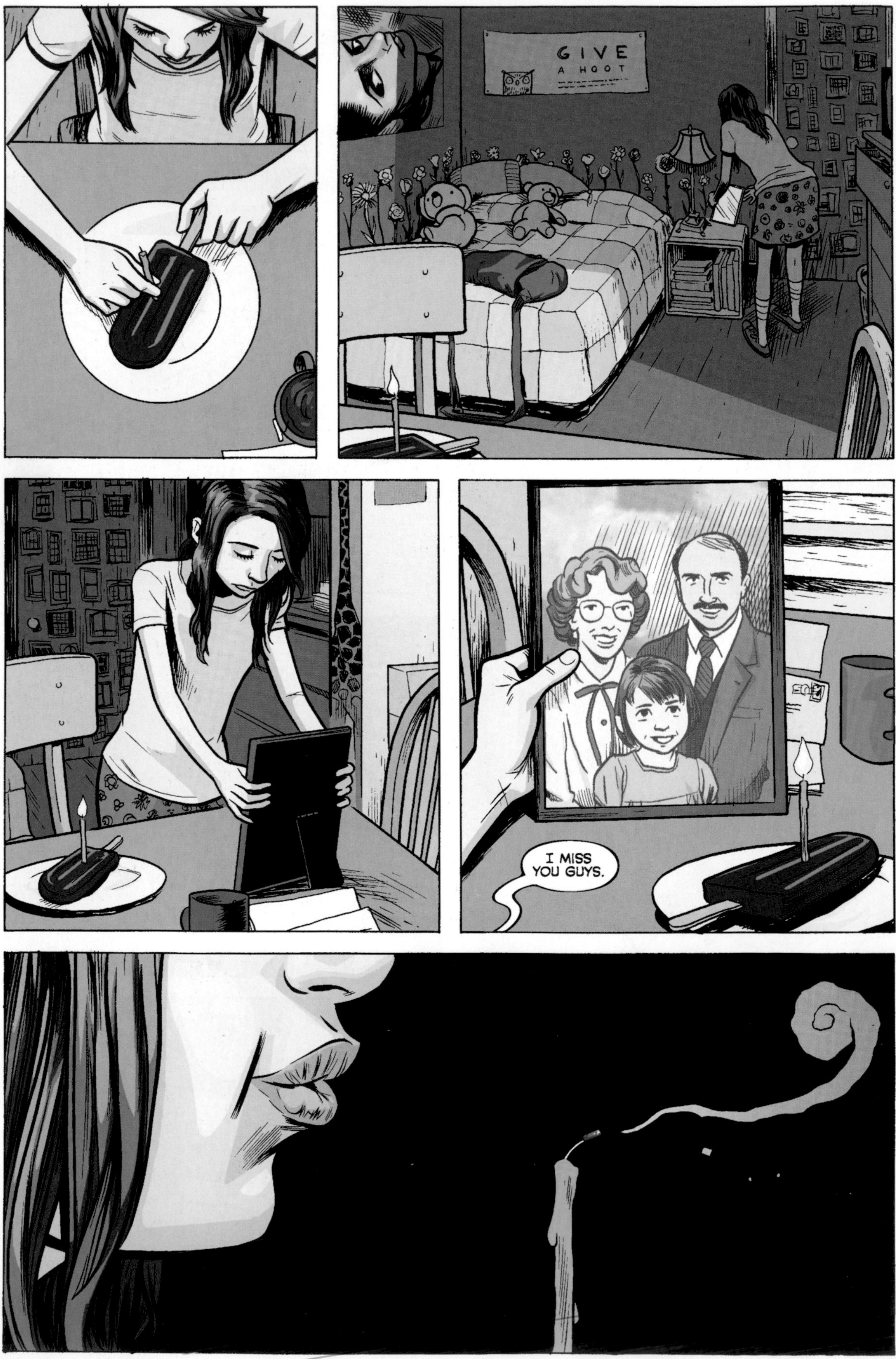
GIVE
A HOOT
I MISS YOU GUYS.

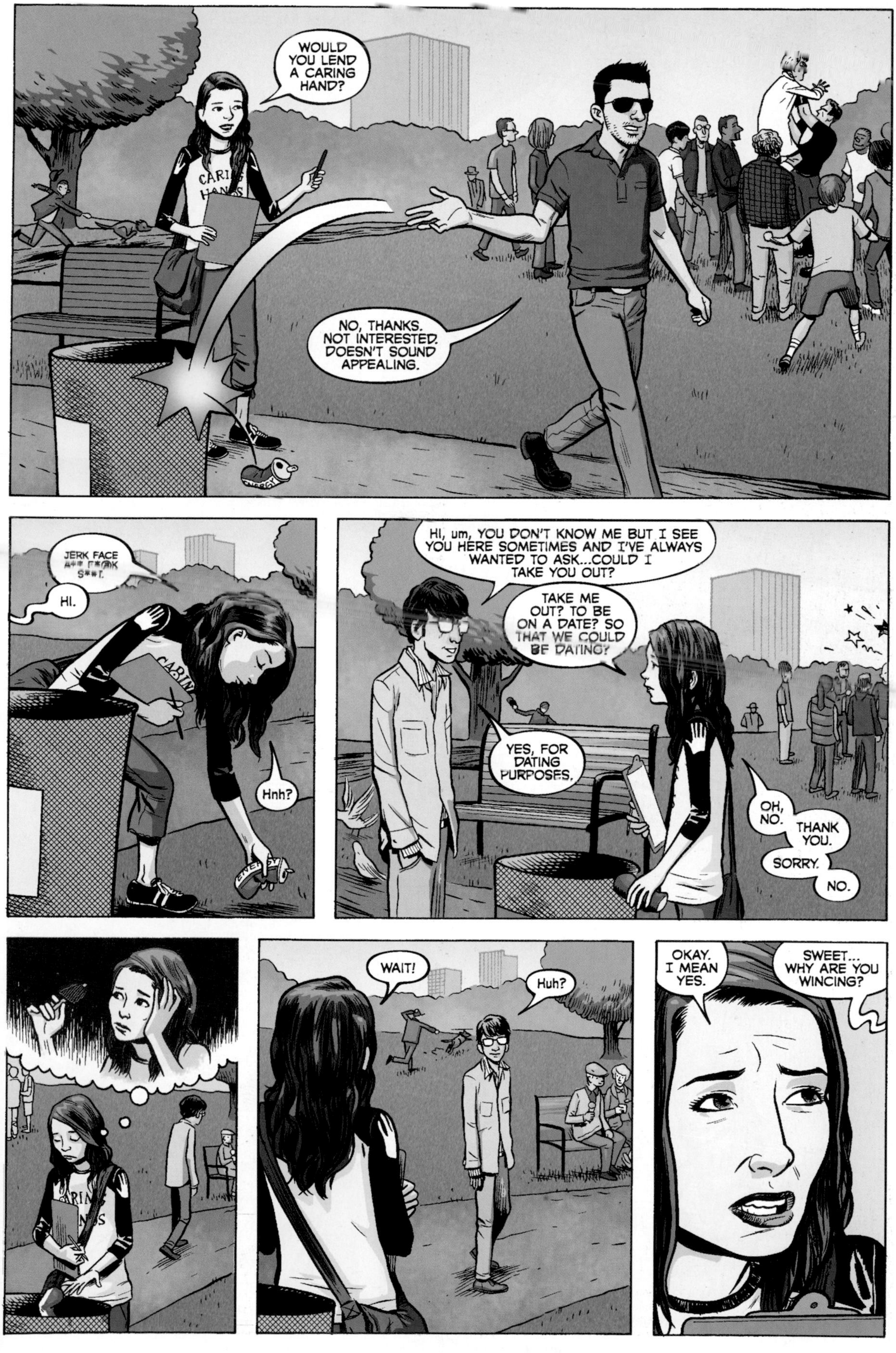
WOULD YOU LEND A CARING HAND?
NO, THANKS. NOT INTERESTED. DOESN'T SOUND APPEALING.
JERK FACE
A** F*@K
S**T.
HI.
Hnh?
HI, um, YOU DON'T KNOW ME BUT I SEE YOU HERE SOMETIMES AND I'VE ALWAYS WANTED TO ASK...COULD I TAKE YOU OUT?
TAKE ME OUT? TO BE ON A DATE? SO THAT WE COULD BE DATING?
YES, FOR DATING PURPOSES.
OH, NO.
THANK YOU.
SORRY.
NO.
WAIT!
Huh?
OKAY. I MEAN YES.
SWEET... WHY ARE YOU WINCING?

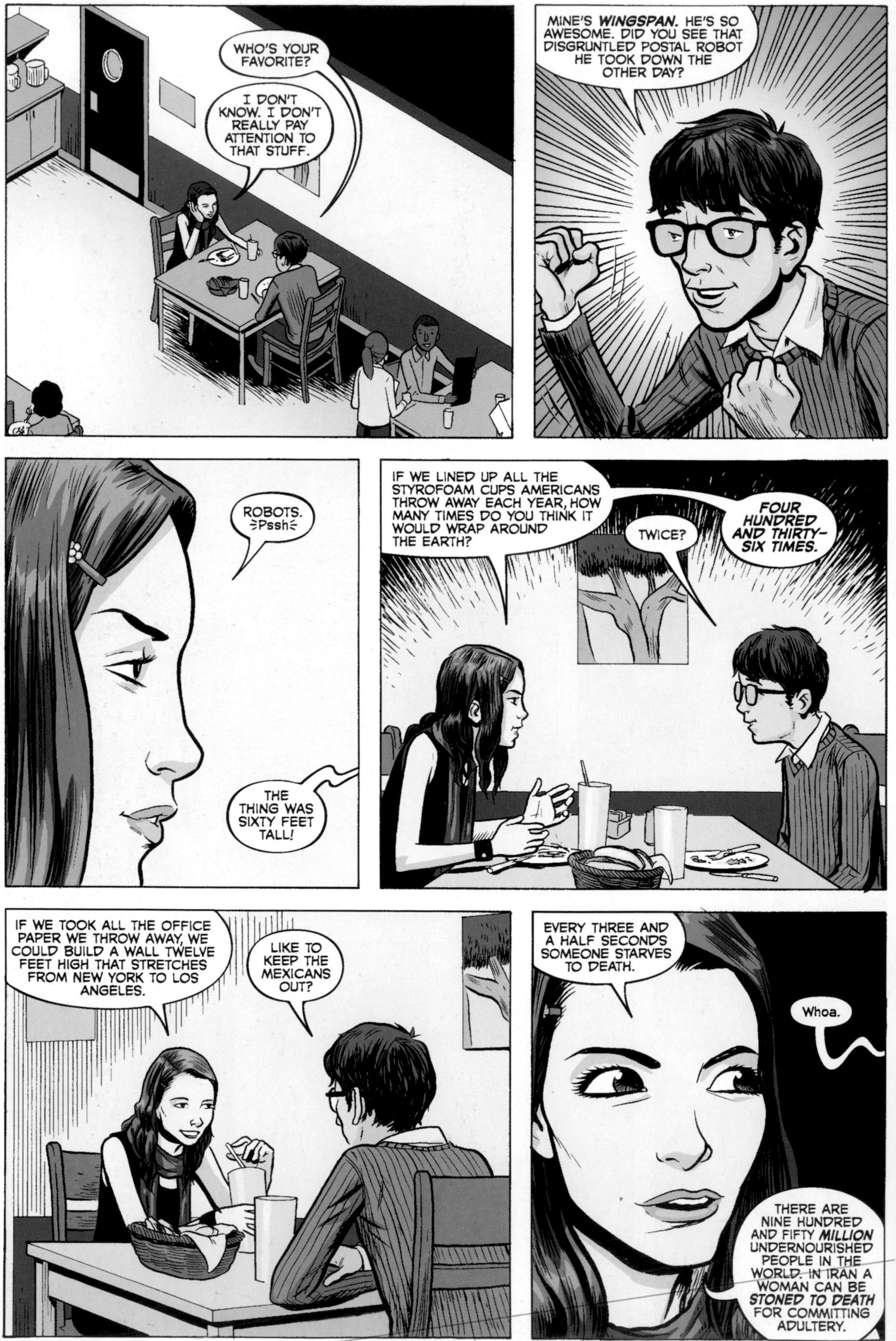
WHO'S YOUR FAVORITE?
I DON'T KNOW. I DON'T REALLY PAY ATTENTION TO THAT STUFF.
MINE'S WINGSPAN. HE'S SO AWESOME. DID YOU SEE THAT DISGRUNTLED POSTAL ROBOT HE TOOK DOWN THE OTHER DAY?
ROBOTS. Pssh
THE THING WAS SIXTY FEET TALL!
IF WE LINED UP ALL THE STYROFOAM CUPS AMERICANS THROW AWAY EACH YEAR, HOW MANY TIMES DO YOU THINK IT WOULD WRAP AROUND THE EARTH?
TWICE?
FOUR HUNDRED AND THIRTY-SIX TIMES.
IF WE TOOK ALL THE OFFICE PAPER WE THROW AWAY, WE COULD BUILD A WALL TWELVE FEET HIGH THAT STRETCHES FROM NEW YORK TO LOS ANGELES.
LIKE TO KEEP THE MEXICANS OUT?
EVERY THREE AND A HALF SECONDS SOMEONE STARVES TO DEATH.
Whoa.
THERE ARE NINE HUNDRED AND FIFTY MILLION UNDERNOURISHED PEOPLE IN THE WORLD. IN IRAN A WOMAN CAN BE STONED TO DEATH FOR COMMITTING ADULTERY.

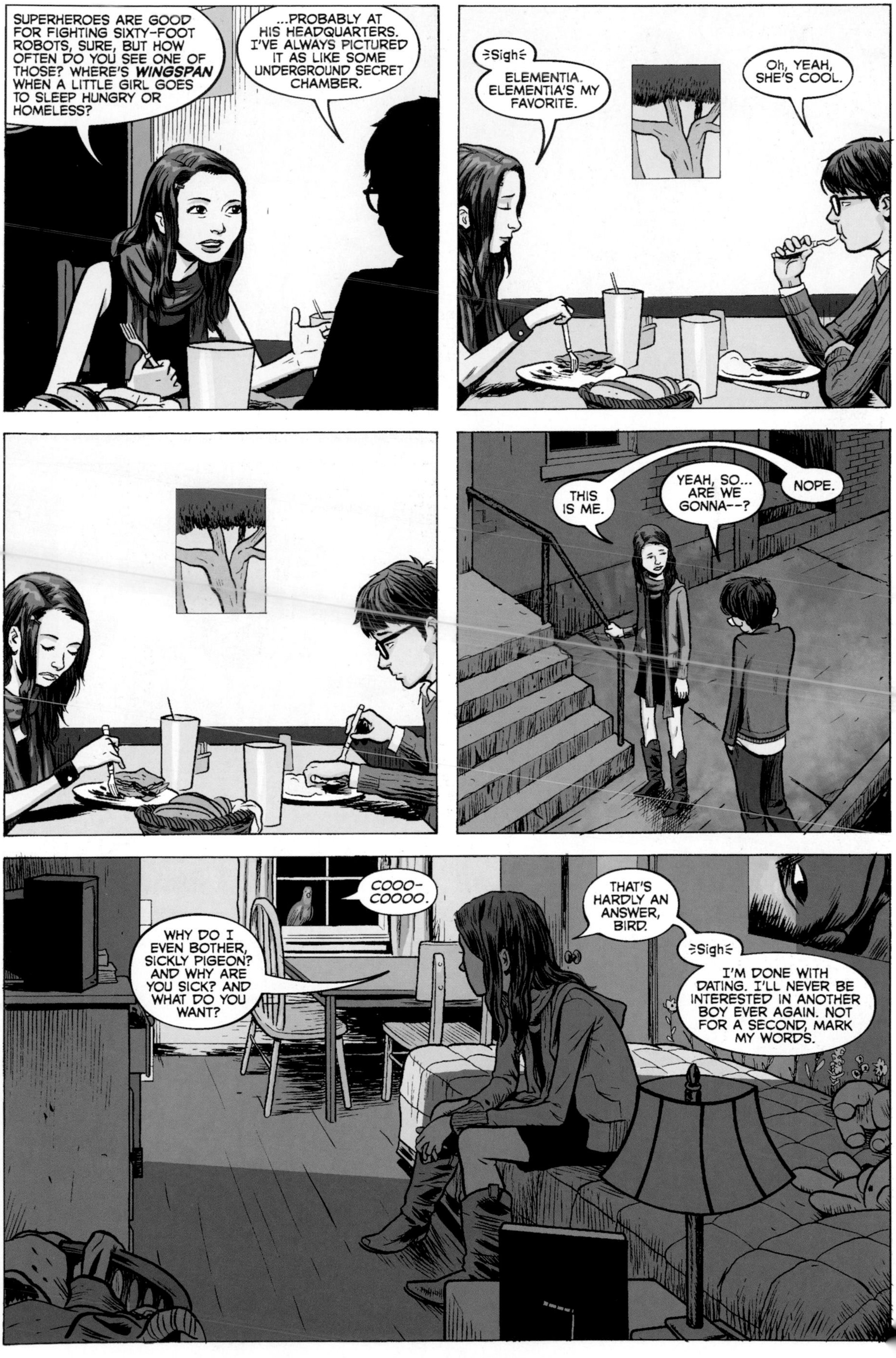
SUPERHEROES ARE GOOD FOR FIGHTING SIXTY-FOOT ROBOTS, SURE, BUT HOW OFTEN DO YOU SEE ONE OF THOSE? WHERE'S WINGSPAN WHEN A LITTLE GIRL GOES TO SLEEP HUNGRY OR HOMELESS?
...PROBABLY AT HIS HEADQUARTERS. I'VE ALWAYS PICTURED IT AS LIKE SOME UNDERGROUND SECRET CHAMBER.
Sigh
ELEMENTIA. ELEMENTIA'S MY FAVORITE.
Oh, YEAH, SHE'S COOL.
THIS IS ME.
YEAH, SO... ARE WE GONNA--?
NOPE.
COOO-COOOO.
WHY DO I EVEN BOTHER, SICKLY PIGEON? AND WHY ARE YOU SICK? AND WHAT DO YOU WANT?
THAT'S HARDLY AN ANSWER, BIRD.
Sigh
I'M DONE WITH DATING. I'LL NEVER BE INTERESTED IN ANOTHER BOY EVER AGAIN. NOT FOR A SECOND, MARK MY WORDS.

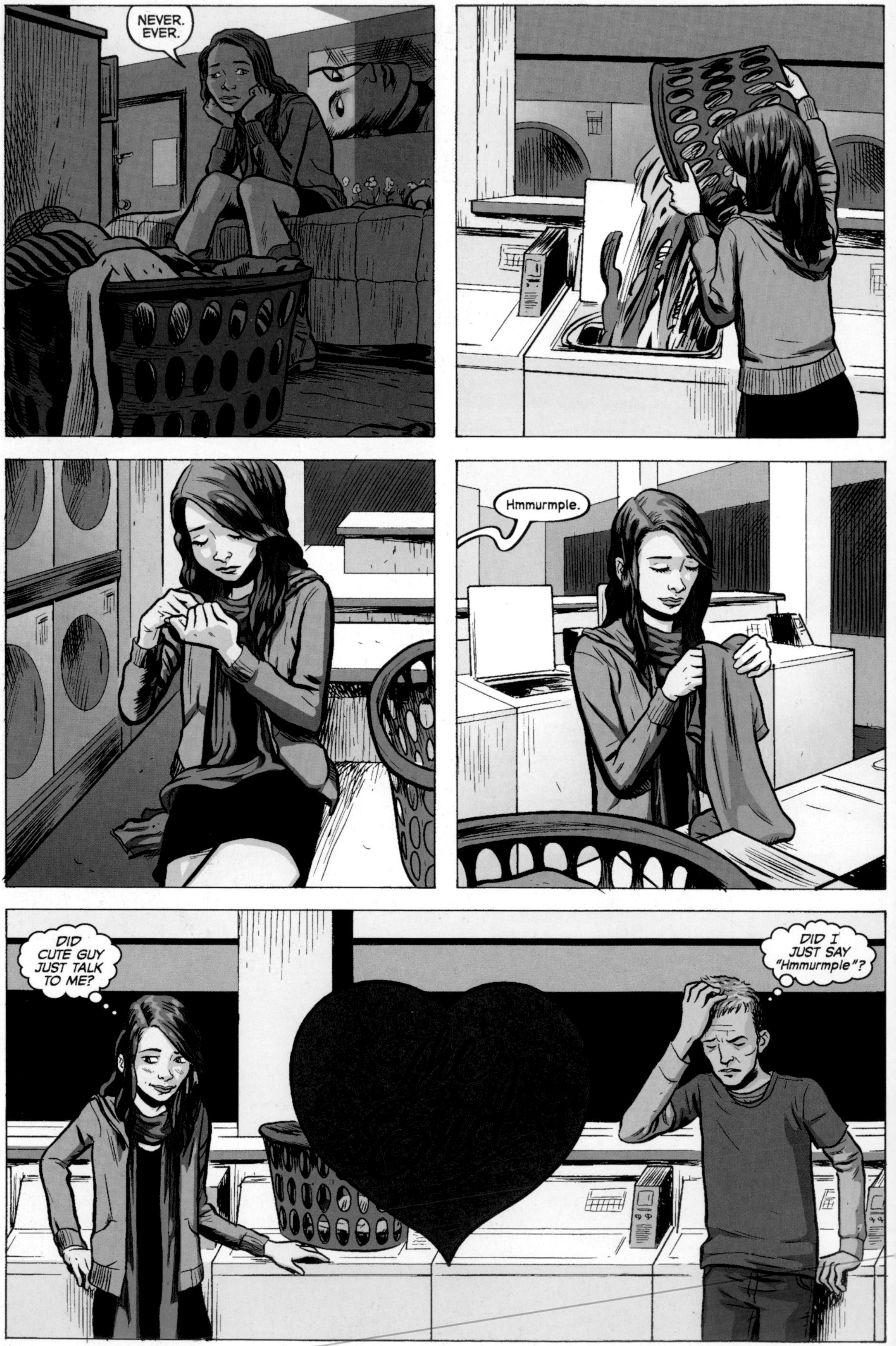
NEVER. EVER.
Hmmurmple.
DID CUTE GUY JUST TALK TO ME?
DID I JUST SAY "Hmmurmple"?

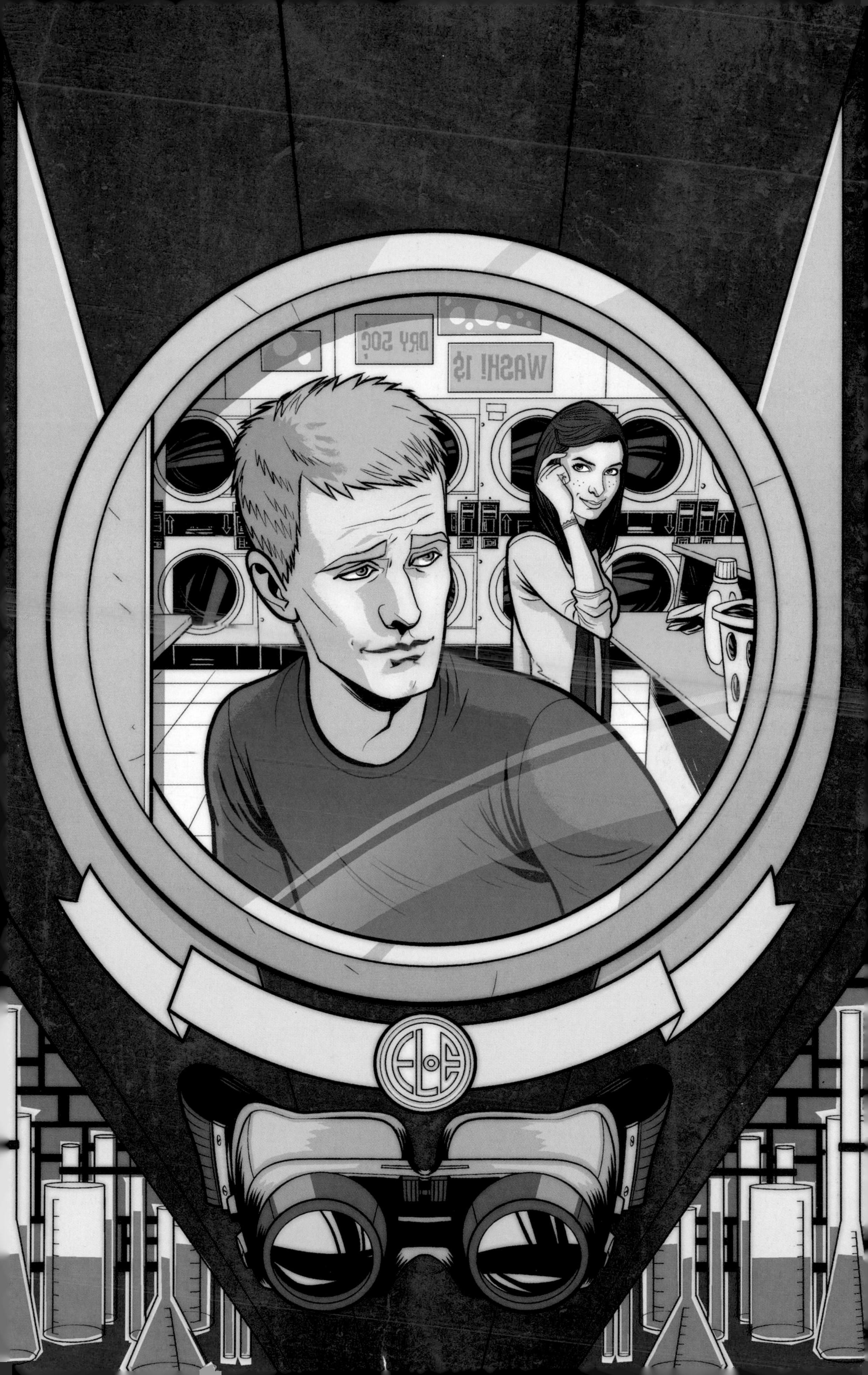

THE EVIL LEAGUE OF EVIL

Story by
ZACK WHEDON

Art by
SCOTT HEPBURN

Colors by
DAN JACKSON

Letters by
NATE PIEKOS OF BLAMBOT®

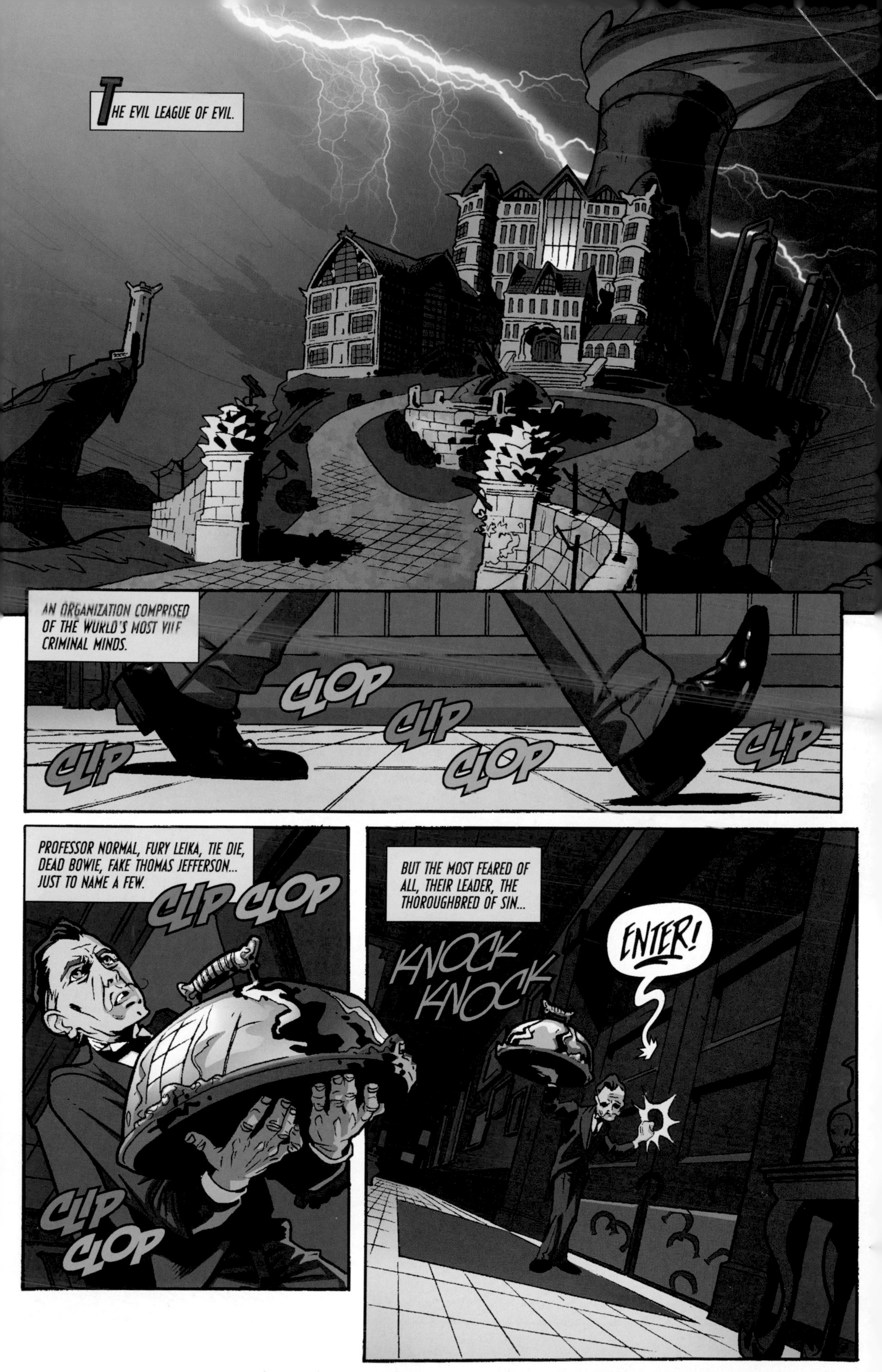
THE EVIL LEAGUE OF EVIL.
AN ORGANIZATION COMPRISED OF THE WORLD'S MOST VILE CRIMINAL MINDS.
CLOP
CLIP
CLIP
CLOP
CLIP
PROFESSOR NORMAL, FURY LEIKA, TIE DIE, DEAD BOWIE, FAKE THOMAS JEFFERSON... JUST TO NAME A FEW.
CLIP CLOP
CLIP
CLOP
BUT THE MOST FEARED OF ALL, THEIR LEADER, THE THOROUGHBRED OF SIN...
KNOCK
KNOCK
ENTER!

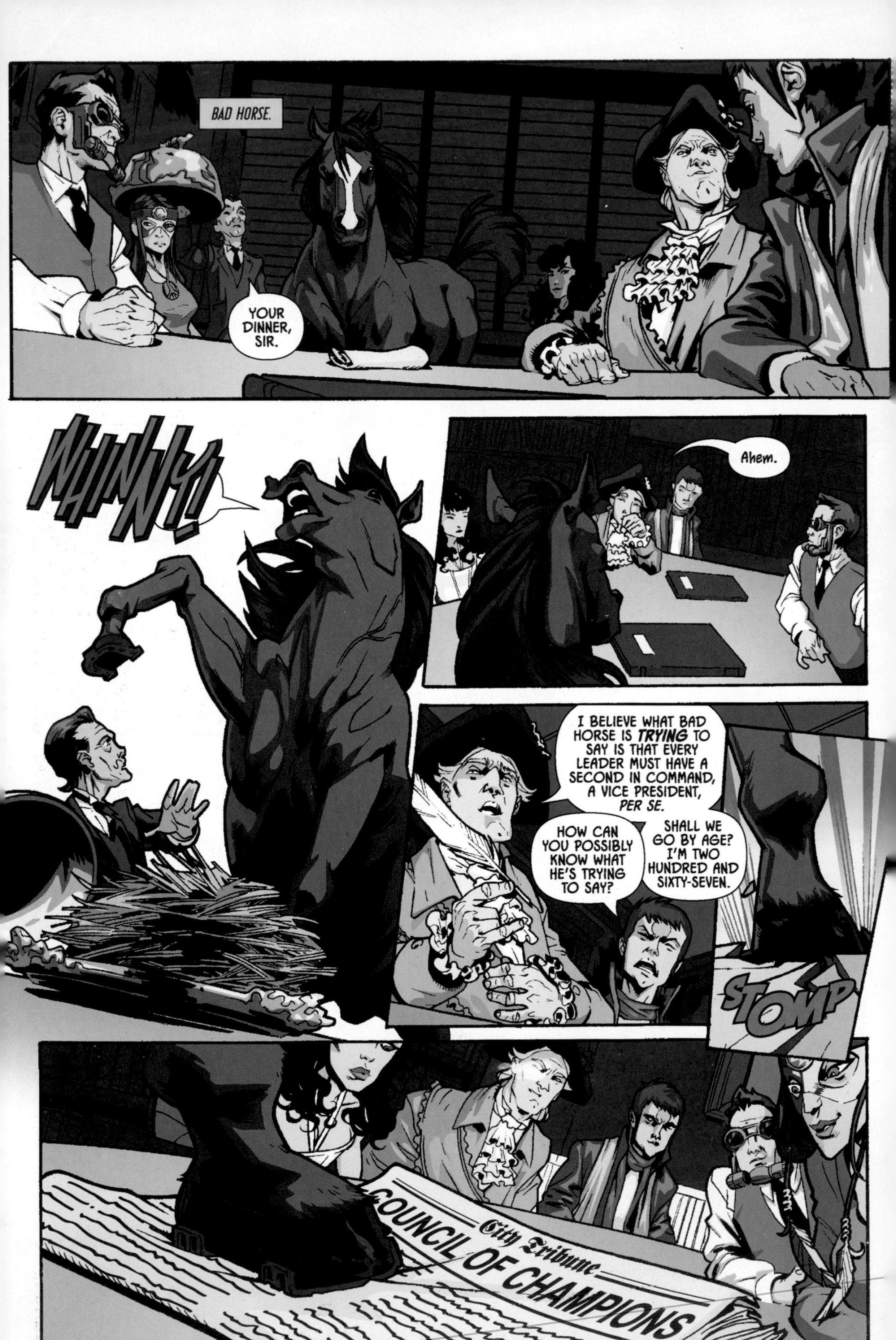
BAD HORSE.
YOUR DINNER, SIR.
NUHNNY!
Ahem.
I BELIEVE WHAT BAD HORSE IS TRYING TO SAY IS THAT EVERY LEADER MUST HAVE A SECOND IN COMMAND, A VICE PRESIDENT, PER SE.
HOW CAN YOU POSSIBLY KNOW WHAT HE'S TRYING TO SAY?
SHALL WE GO BY AGE? I'M TWO HUNDRED AND SIXTY-SEVEN.
STOMP
City Tribune
COUNCIL OF CHAMPIONS

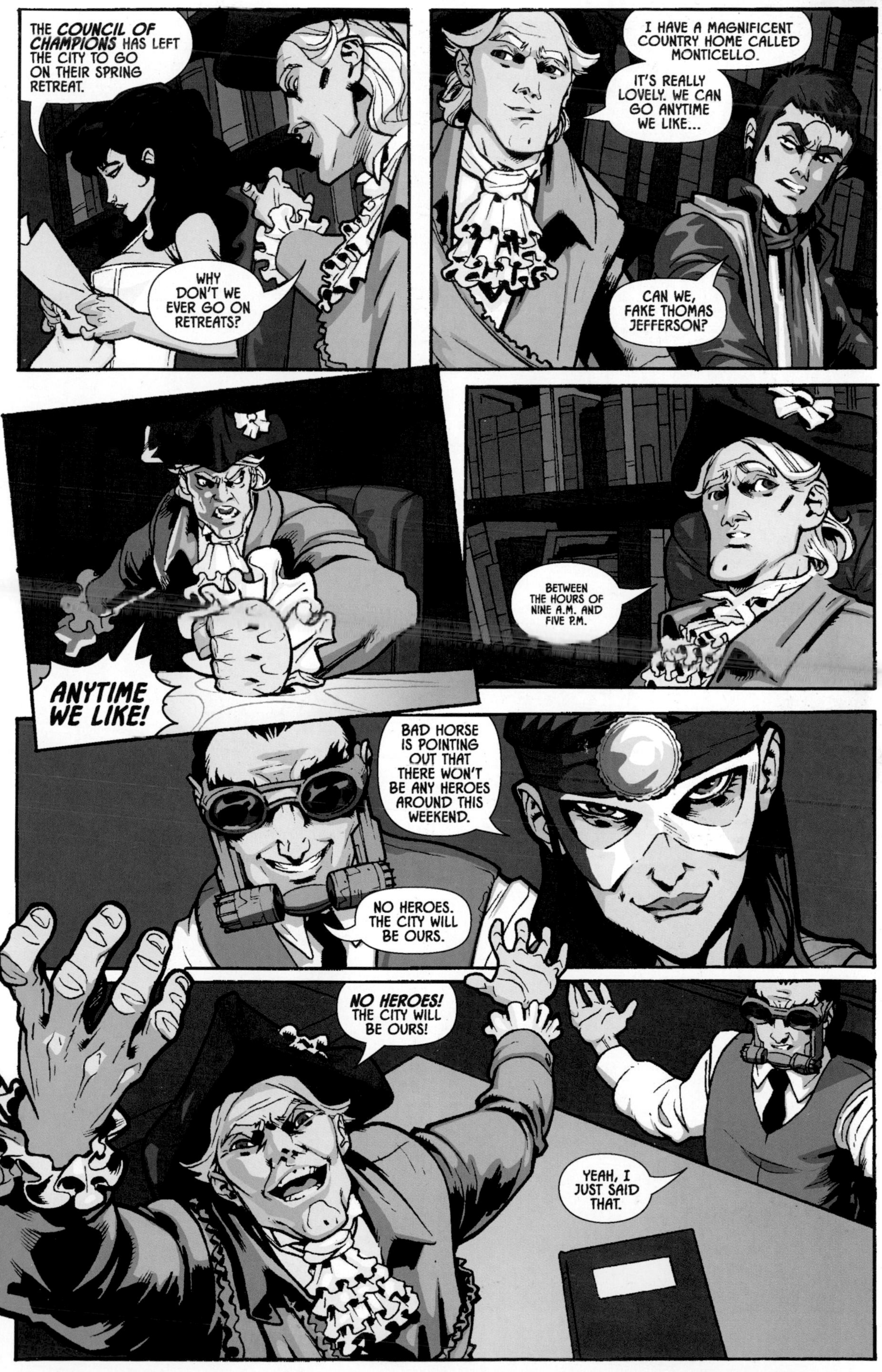
THE *COUNCIL OF CHAMPIONS* HAS LEFT THE CITY TO GO ON THEIR SPRING RETREAT.
WHY DON'T WE EVER GO ON RETREATS?
I HAVE A MAGNIFICENT COUNTRY HOME CALLED MONTICELLO.
IT'S REALLY LOVELY. WE CAN GO ANYTIME WE LIKE...
CAN WE, FAKE THOMAS JEFFERSON?
ANYTIME WE LIKE!
BETWEEN THE HOURS OF NINE A.M. AND FIVE P.M.
BAD HORSE IS POINTING OUT THAT THERE WON'T BE ANY HEROES AROUND THIS WEEKEND.
NO HEROES. THE CITY WILL BE OURS.
NO HEROES! THE CITY WILL BE OURS!
YEAH, I JUST SAID THAT.

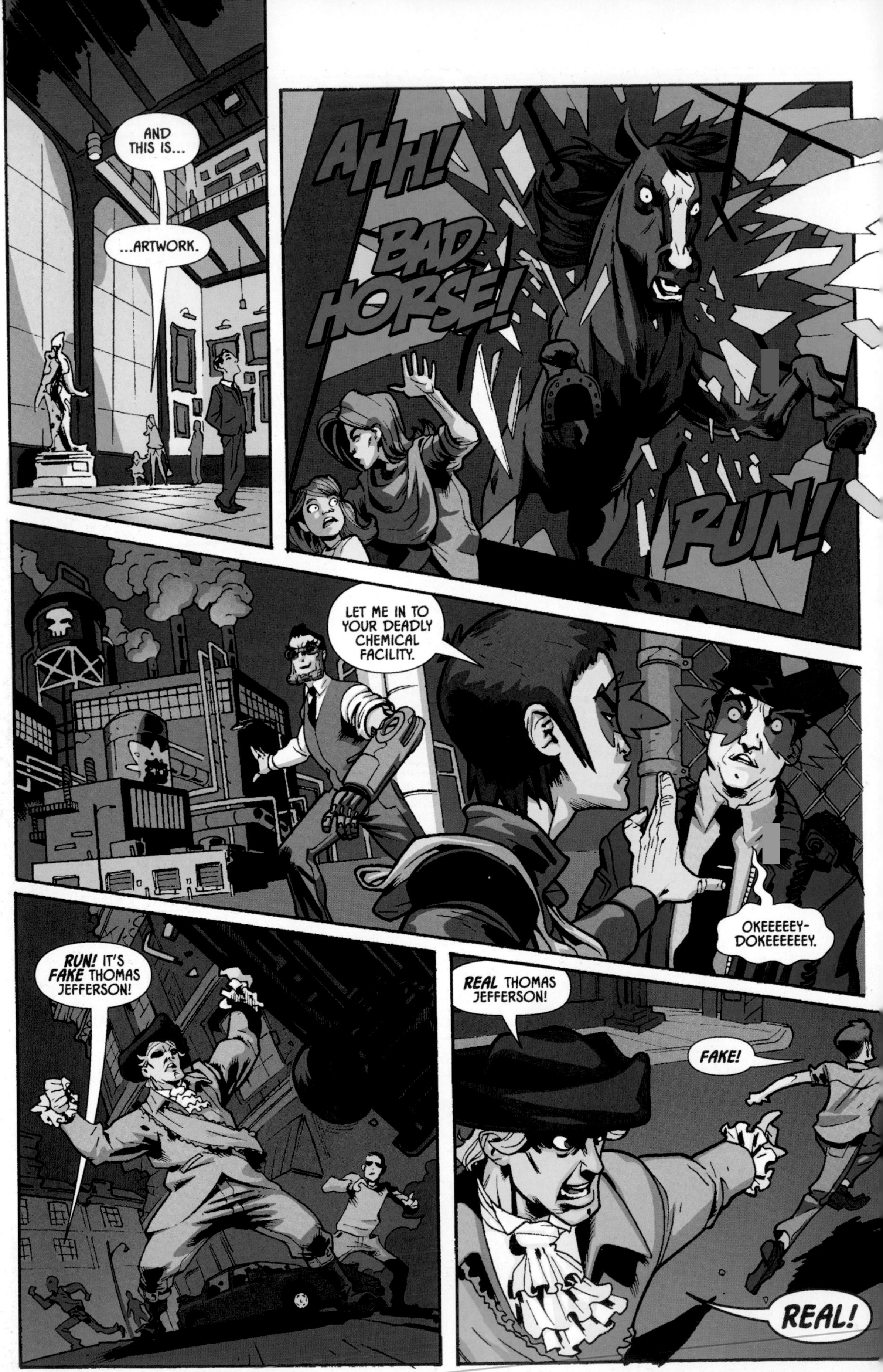
AND THIS IS...
...ARTWORK.
AHH!
BAD HORSE!
RUN!
LET ME IN TO YOUR DEADLY CHEMICAL FACILITY.
OKEEEEEY-DOKEEEEEEY.
RUN! IT'S FAKE THOMAS JEFFERSON!
REAL THOMAS JEFFERSON!
FAKE!
REAL!

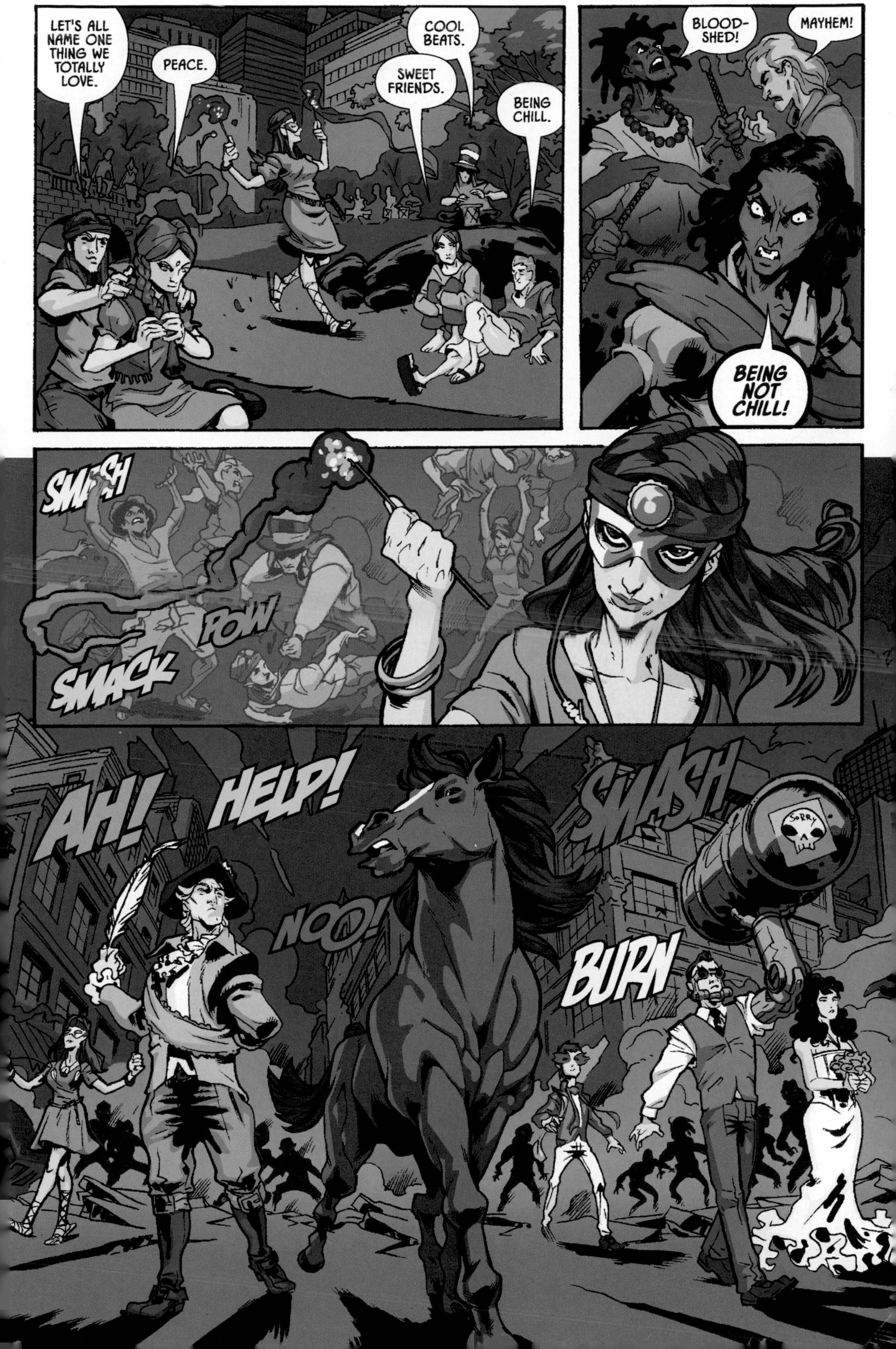
LET'S ALL NAME ONE THING WE TOTALLY LOVE.
PEACE.
COOL BEATS.
SWEET FRIENDS.
BEING CHILL.
BLOOD-SHED!
MAYHEM!
BEING NOT CHILL!
SMASH
POW
SMACK
AH!
HELP!
NOO!
SMASH
SORRY
BURN

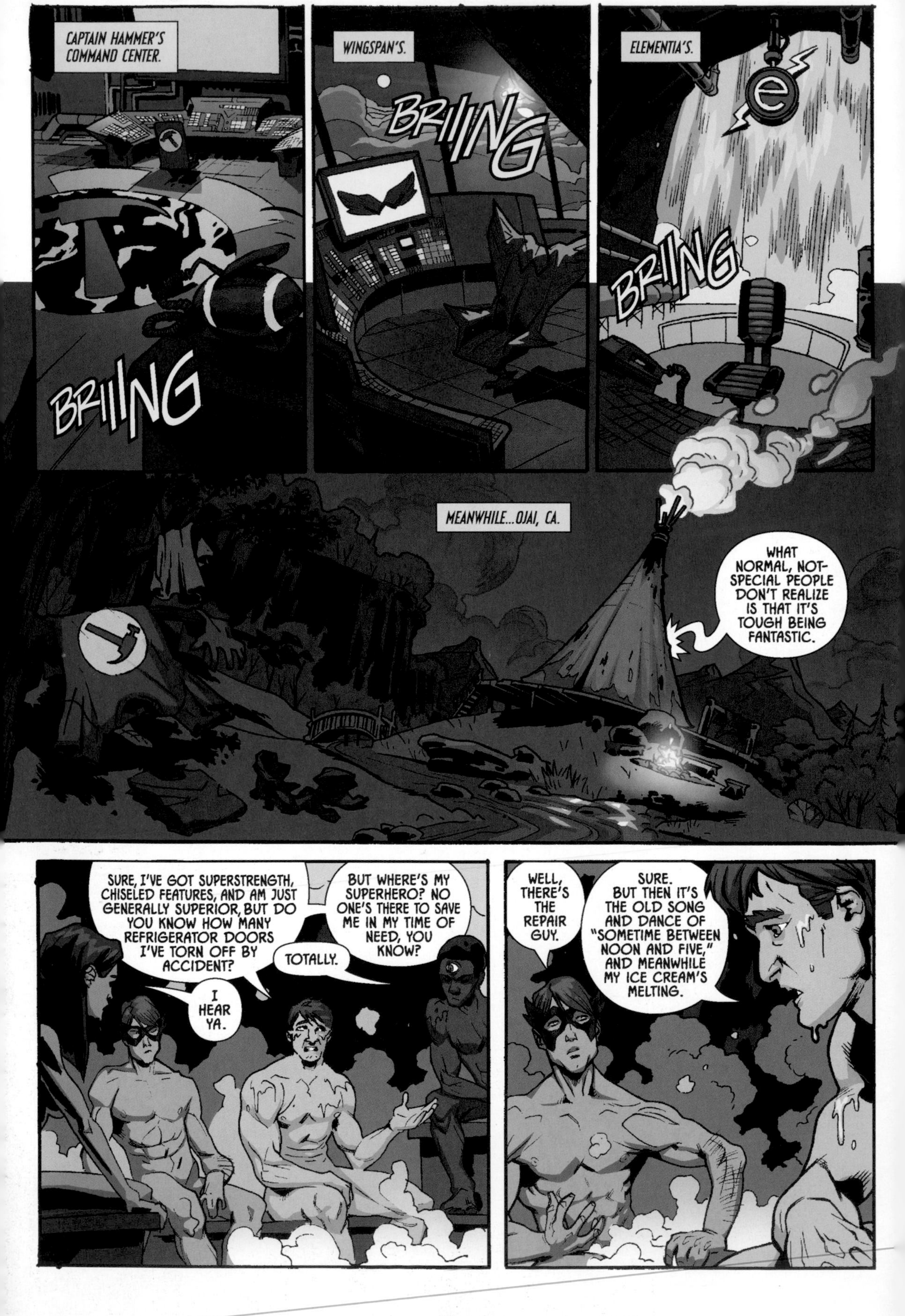
CAPTAIN HAMMER'S COMMAND CENTER.
BRIIING
WINGSPAN'S.
BRIIING
ELEMENTIA'S.
BRIING
MEANWHILE...OJAI, CA.
WHAT NORMAL, NOT-SPECIAL PEOPLE DON'T REALIZE IS THAT IT'S TOUGH BEING FANTASTIC.
SURE, I'VE GOT SUPERSTRENGTH, CHISELED FEATURES, AND AM JUST GENERALLY SUPERIOR, BUT DO YOU KNOW HOW MANY REFRIGERATOR DOORS I'VE TORN OFF BY ACCIDENT?
I HEAR YA.
BUT WHERE'S MY SUPERHERO? NO ONE'S THERE TO SAVE ME IN MY TIME OF NEED, YOU KNOW?
TOTALLY.
WELL, THERE'S THE REPAIR GUY.
SURE. BUT THEN IT'S THE OLD SONG AND DANCE OF "SOMETIME BETWEEN NOON AND FIVE," AND MEANWHILE MY ICE CREAM'S MELTING.

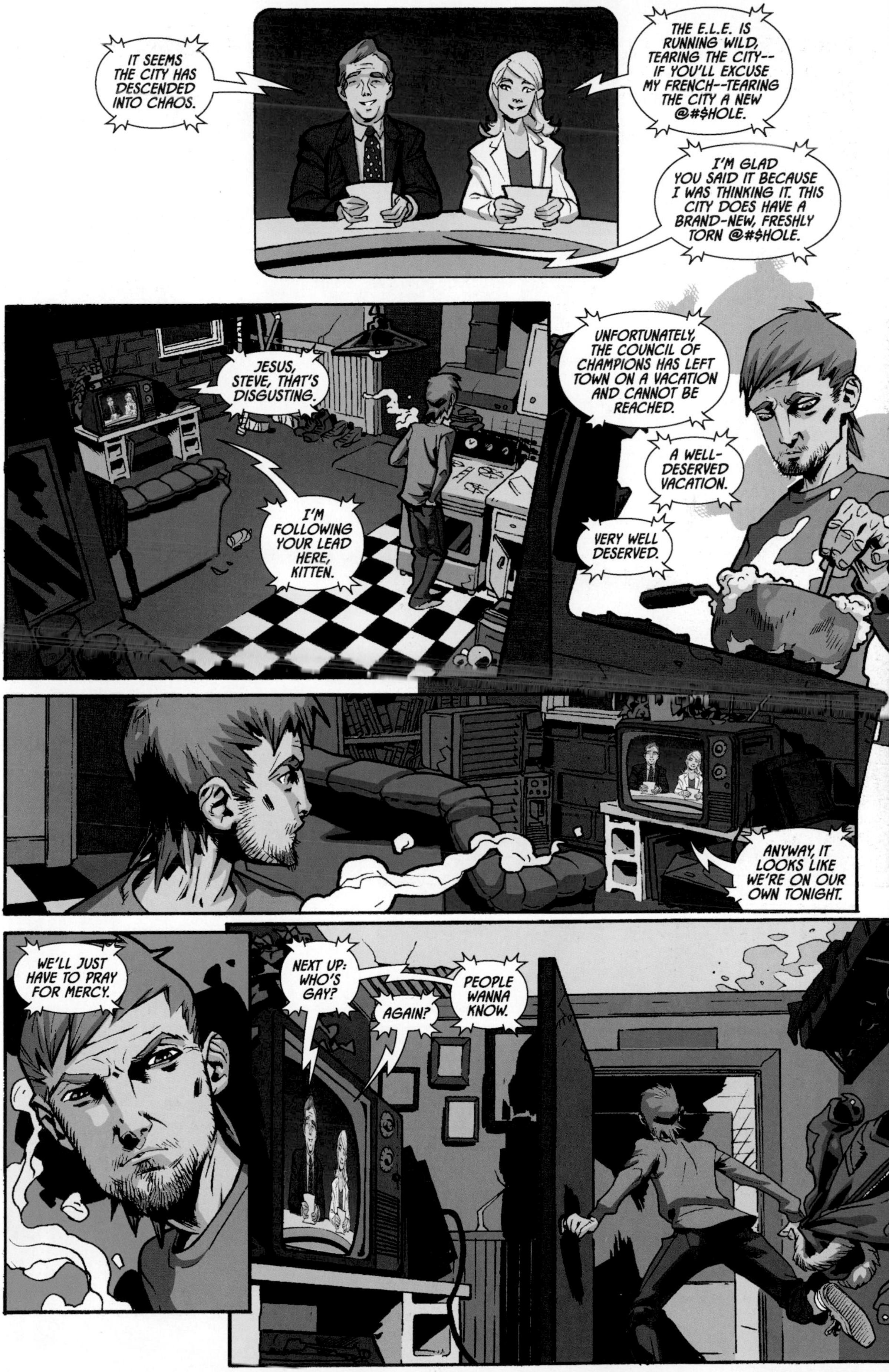
IT SEEMS THE CITY HAS DESCENDED INTO CHAOS.
THE E.L.E. IS RUNNING WILD, TEARING THE CITY-- IF YOU'LL EXCUSE MY FRENCH--TEARING THE CITY A NEW @#$HOLE.
I'M GLAD YOU SAID IT BECAUSE I WAS THINKING IT. THIS CITY DOES HAVE A BRAND-NEW, FRESHLY TORN @#$HOLE.
JESUS, STEVE, THAT'S DISGUSTING.
I'M FOLLOWING YOUR LEAD HERE, KITTEN.
UNFORTUNATELY, THE COUNCIL OF CHAMPIONS HAS LEFT TOWN ON A VACATION AND CANNOT BE REACHED.
A WELL-DESERVED VACATION.
VERY WELL DESERVED.
ANYWAY, IT LOOKS LIKE WE'RE ON OUR OWN TONIGHT.
WE'LL JUST HAVE TO PRAY FOR MERCY.
NEXT UP: WHO'S GAY?
AGAIN?
PEOPLE WANNA KNOW.

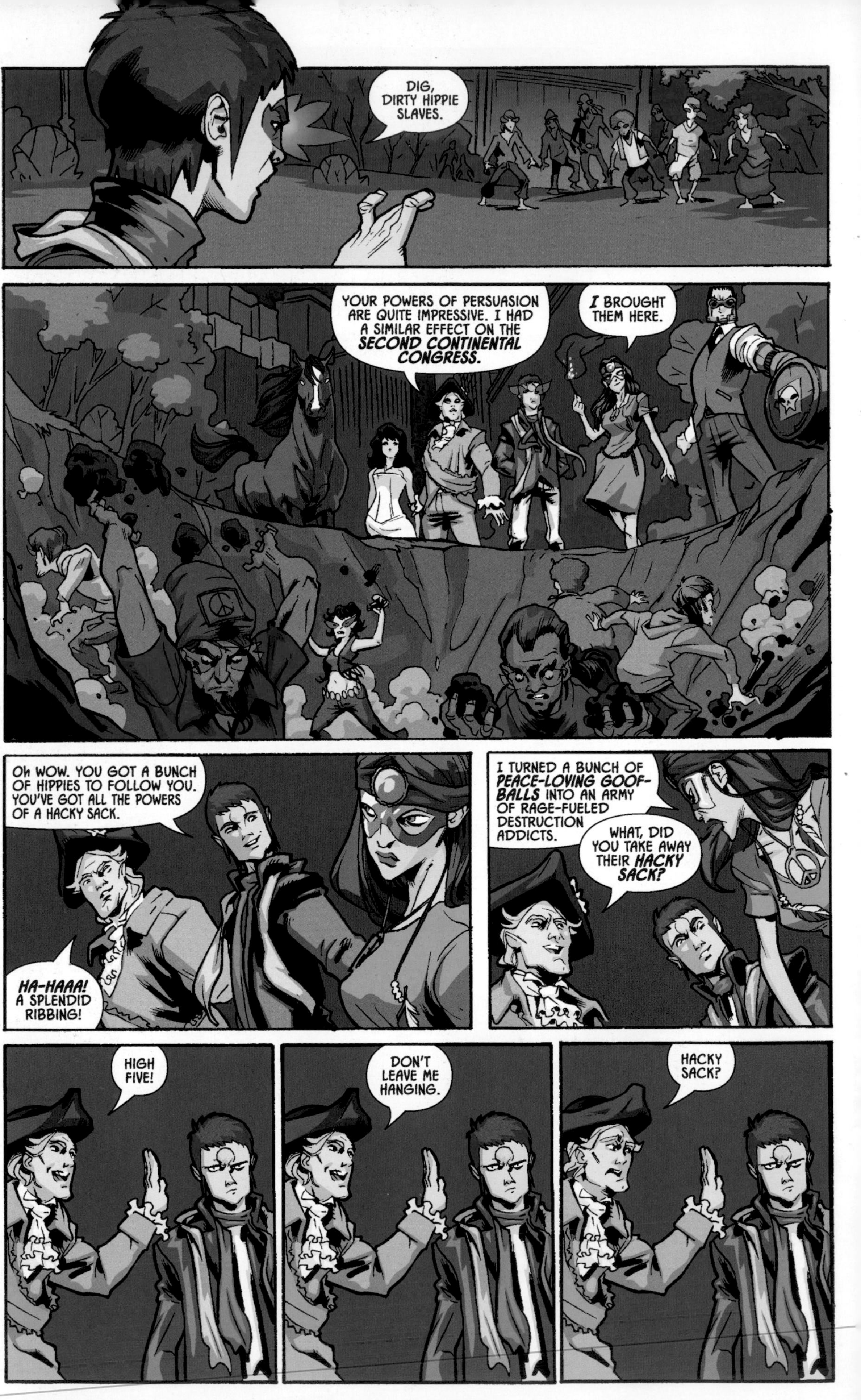
DIG, DIRTY HIPPIE SLAVES.
YOUR POWERS OF PERSUASION ARE QUITE IMPRESSIVE. I HAD A SIMILAR EFFECT ON THE SECOND CONTINENTAL CONGRESS.
I BROUGHT THEM HERE.
Oh WOW. YOU GOT A BUNCH OF HIPPIES TO FOLLOW YOU. YOU'VE GOT ALL THE POWERS OF A HACKY SACK.
HA-HAAA! A SPLENDID RIBBING!
I TURNED A BUNCH OF PEACE-LOVING GOOF-BALLS INTO AN ARMY OF RAGE-FUELED DESTRUCTION ADDICTS.
WHAT, DID YOU TAKE AWAY THEIR HACKY SACK?
HIGH FIVE!
DON'T LEAVE ME HANGING.
HACKY SACK?

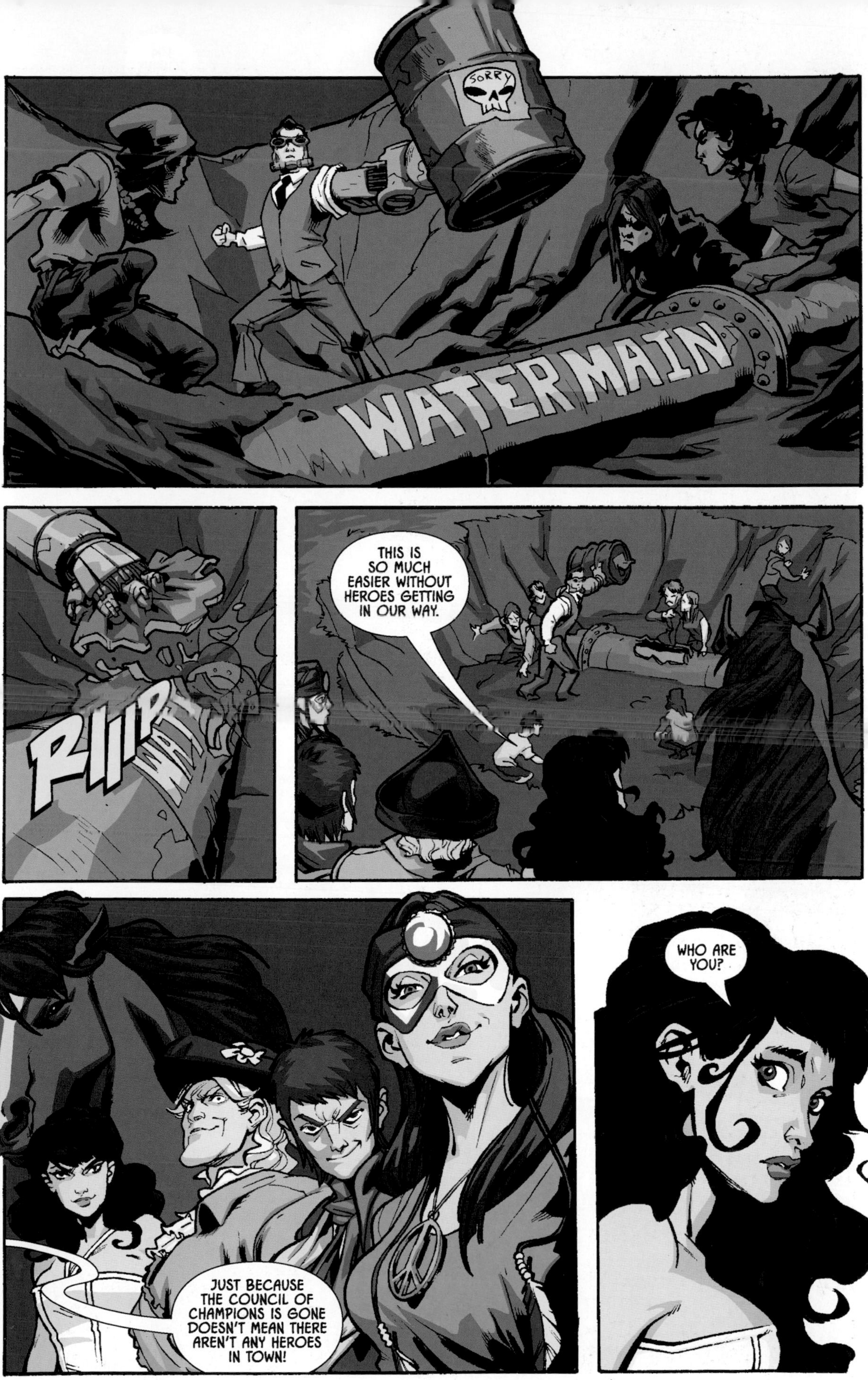
SORRY
WATERMAIN
RIIIP
THIS IS SO MUCH EASIER WITHOUT HEROES GETTING IN OUR WAY.
JUST BECAUSE THE COUNCIL OF CHAMPIONS IS GONE DOESN'T MEAN THERE AREN'T ANY HEROES IN TOWN!
WHO ARE YOU?

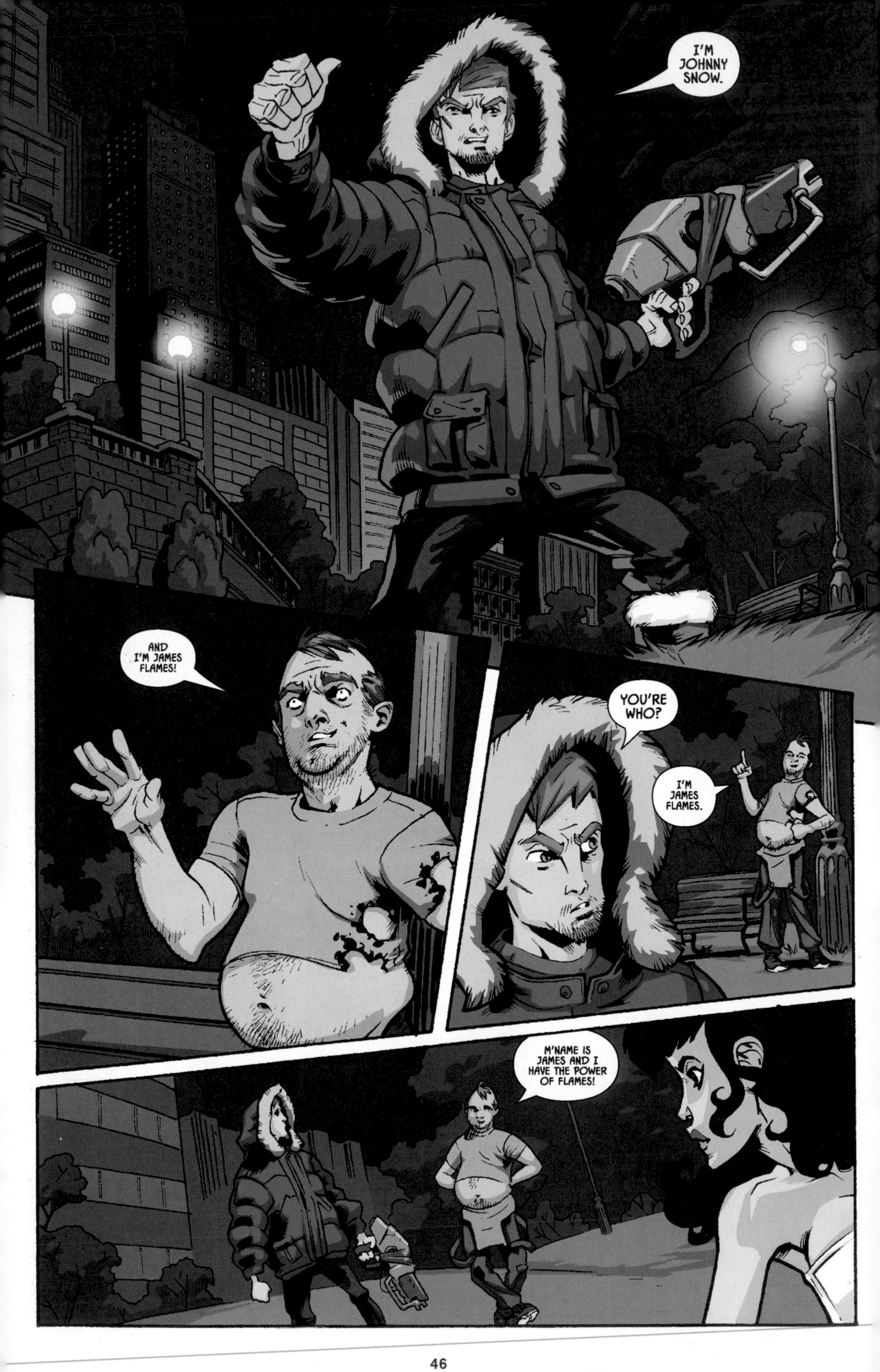

I'M JOHNNY SNOW.
AND I'M JAMES FLAMES!
YOU'RE WHO?
I'M JAMES FLAMES.
M'NAME IS JAMES AND I HAVE THE POWER OF FLAMES!

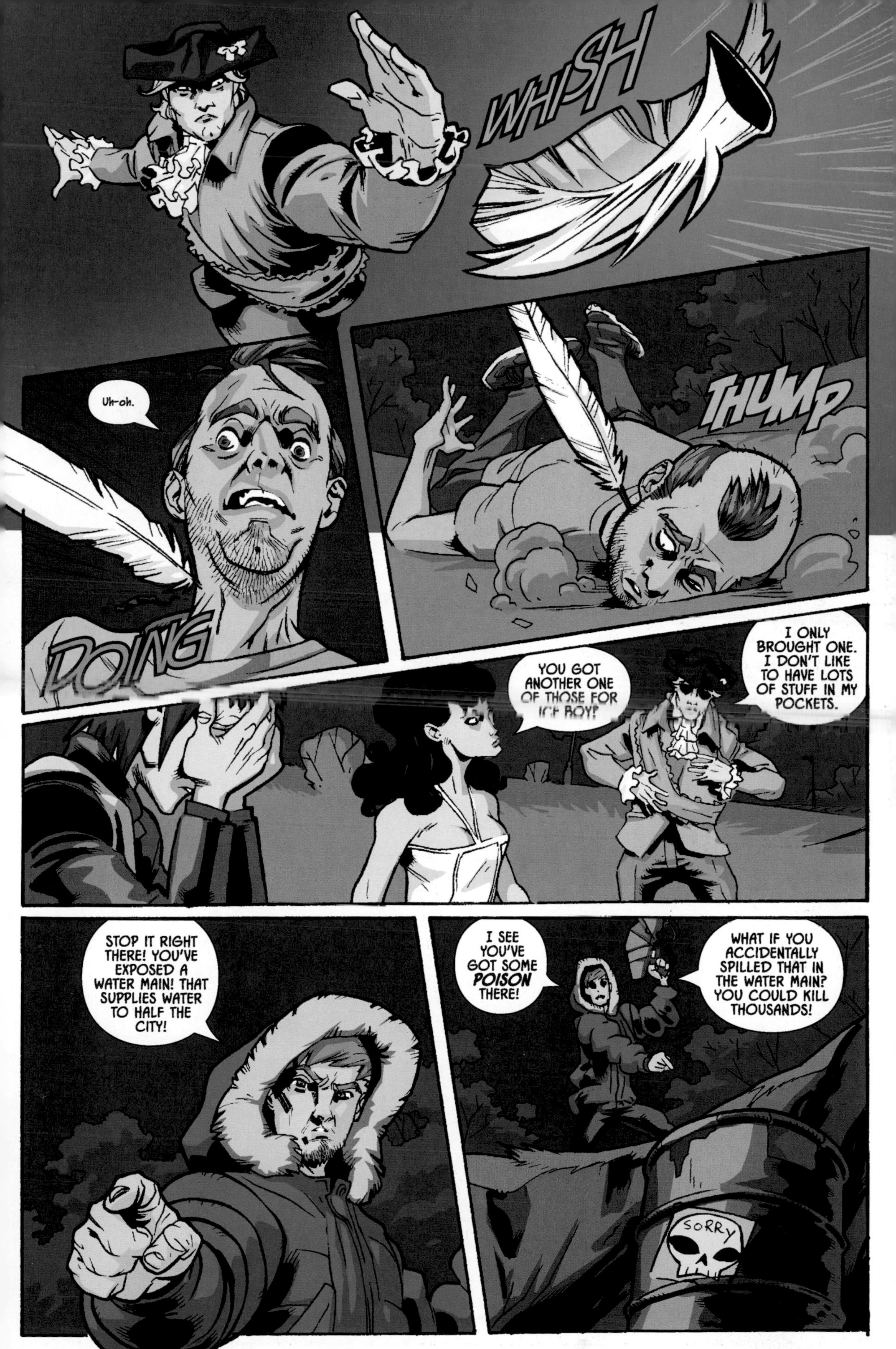
WHISH
Uh-oh.
DOING
THUMP
YOU GOT ANOTHER ONE OF THOSE FOR ICE BOY?
I ONLY BROUGHT ONE. I DON'T LIKE TO HAVE LOTS OF STUFF IN MY POCKETS.
STOP IT RIGHT THERE! YOU'VE EXPOSED A WATER MAIN! THAT SUPPLIES WATER TO HALF THE CITY!
I SEE YOU'VE GOT SOME POISON THERE!
WHAT IF YOU ACCIDENTALLY SPILLED THAT IN THE WATER MAIN? YOU COULD KILL THOUSANDS!
SORRY

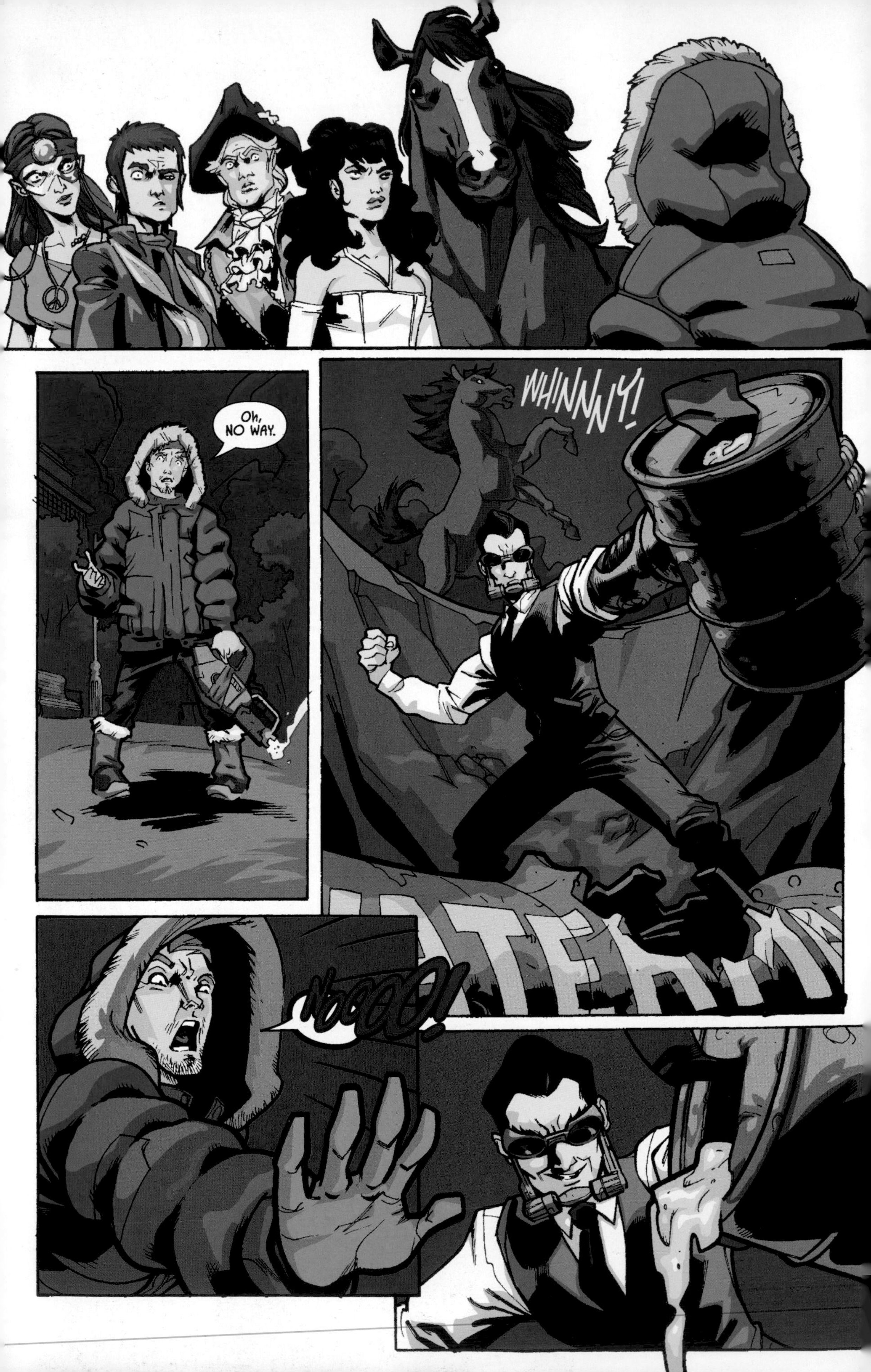
Oh, NO WAY.
WHINNNY!
NOOOO!

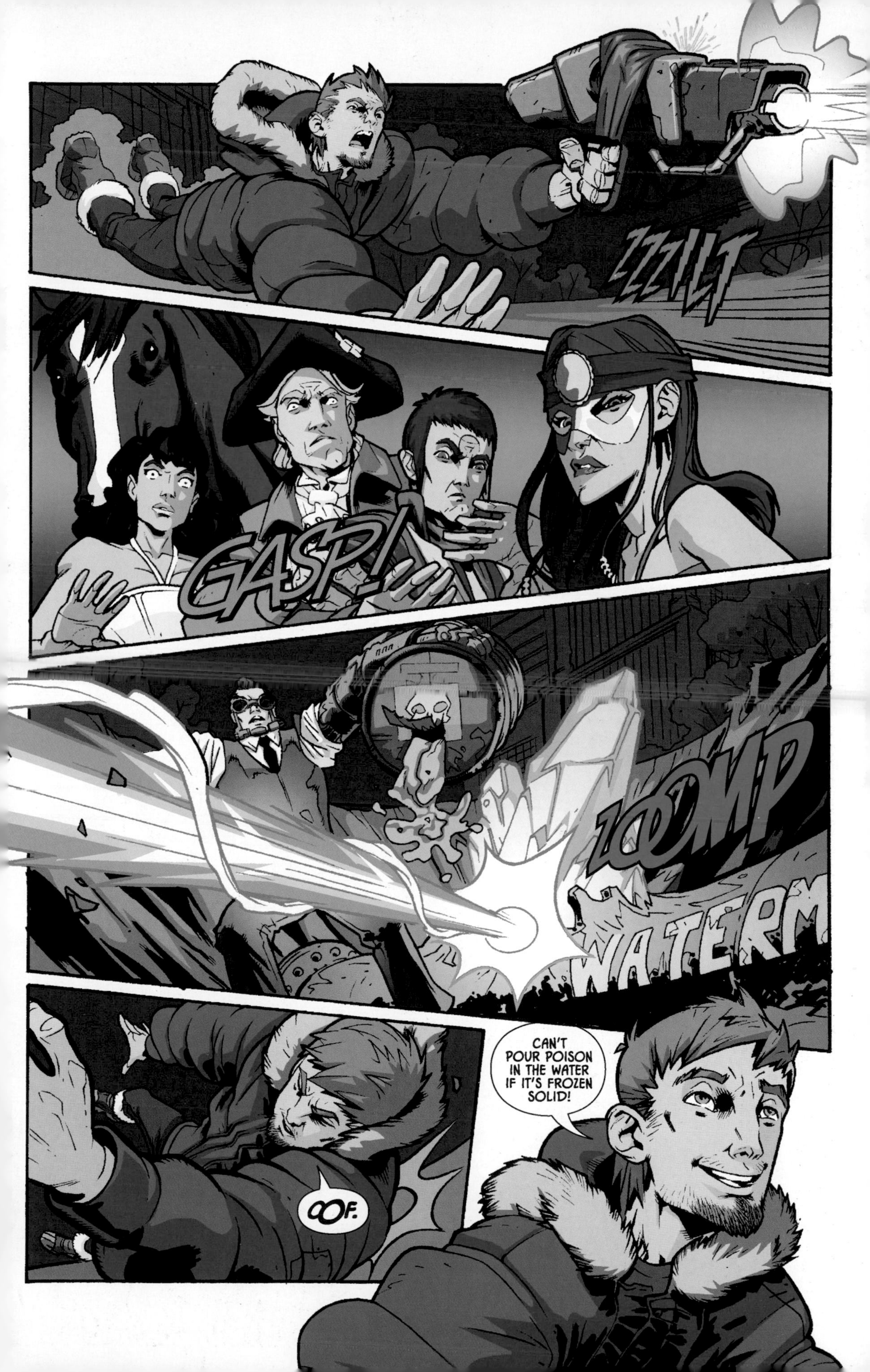
ZZZZLT
GASP!
WOOMP
WATERM
CAN'T POUR POISON IN THE WATER IF IT'S FROZEN SOLID!
OOF.

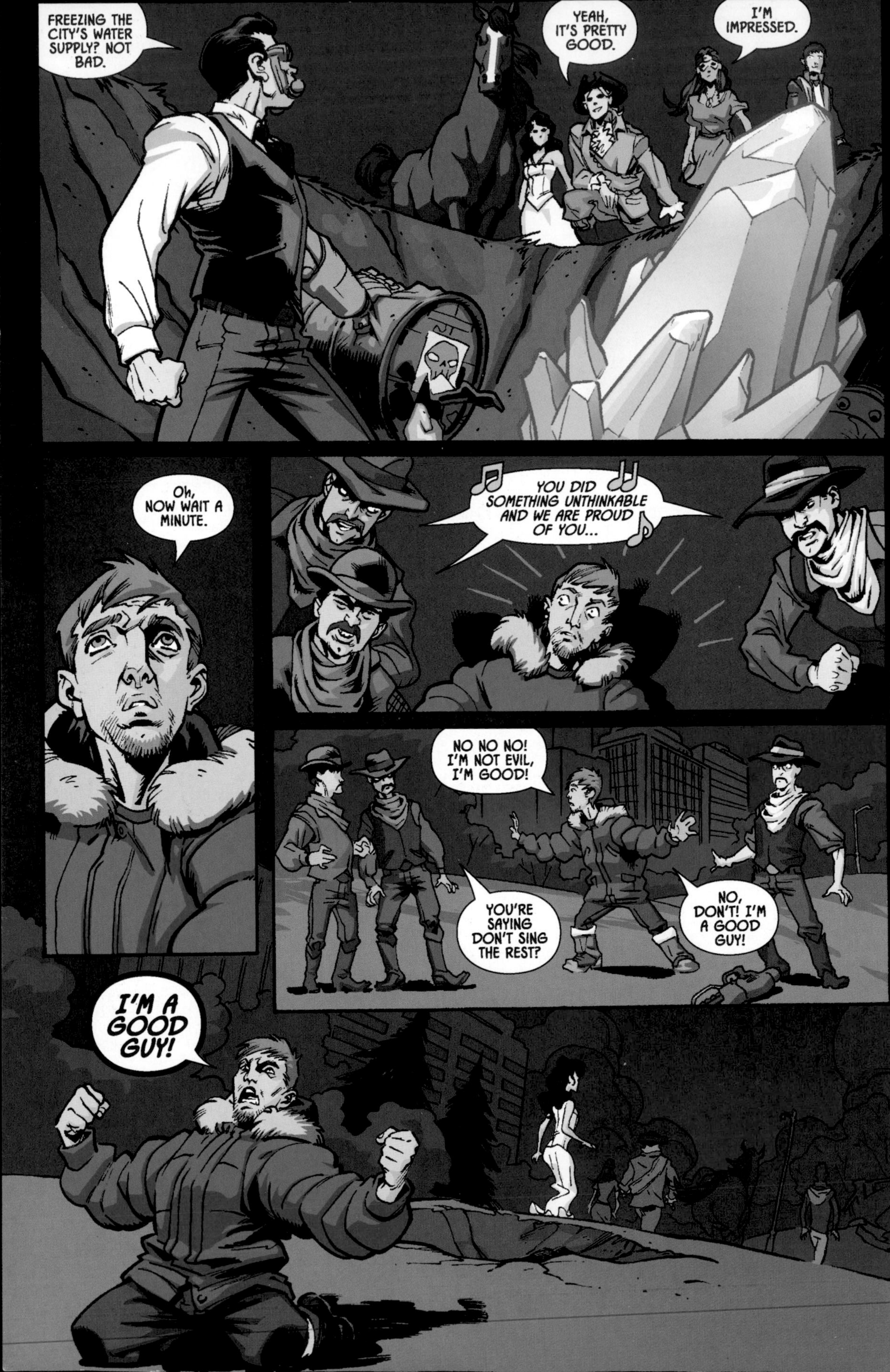
FREEZING THE CITY'S WATER SUPPLY? NOT BAD.
YEAH, IT'S PRETTY GOOD.
I'M IMPRESSED.
Oh, NOW WAIT A MINUTE.
YOU DID SOMETHING UNTHINKABLE AND WE ARE PROUD OF YOU...
NO NO NO! I'M NOT EVIL, I'M GOOD!
YOU'RE SAYING DON'T SING THE REST?
NO, DON'T! I'M A GOOD GUY!
I'M A GOOD GUY!

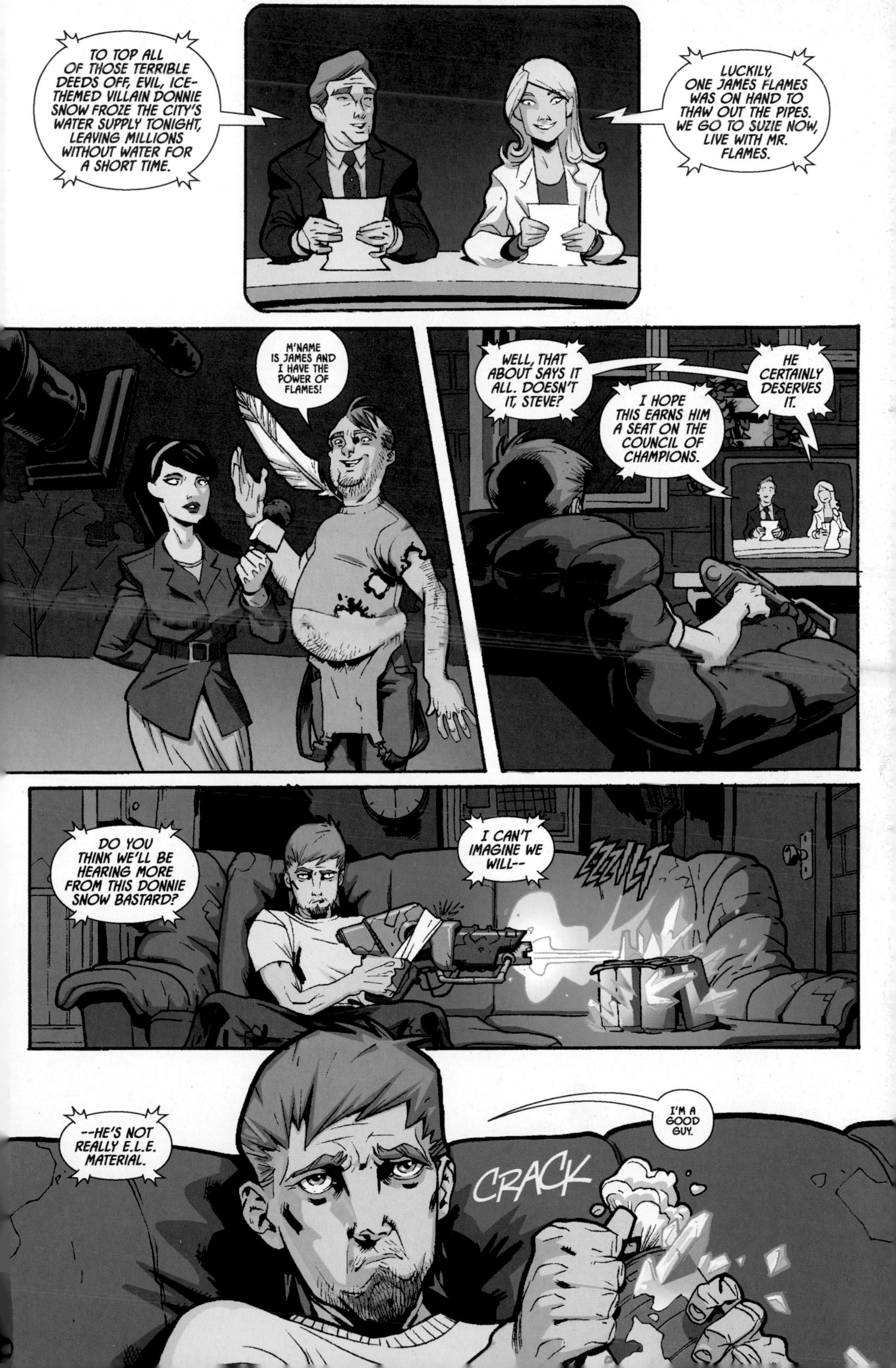
TO TOP ALL OF THOSE TERRIBLE DEEDS OFF, EVIL, ICE-THEMED VILLAIN DONNIE SNOW FROZE THE CITY'S WATER SUPPLY TONIGHT, LEAVING MILLIONS WITHOUT WATER FOR A SHORT TIME.
LUCKILY, ONE JAMES FLAMES WAS ON HAND TO THAW OUT THE PIPES. WE GO TO SUZIE NOW, LIVE WITH MR. FLAMES.
M'NAME IS JAMES AND I HAVE THE POWER OF FLAMES!
WELL, THAT ABOUT SAYS IT ALL. DOESN'T IT, STEVE?
I HOPE THIS EARNS HIM A SEAT ON THE COUNCIL OF CHAMPIONS.
HE CERTAINLY DESERVES IT.
DO YOU THINK WE'LL BE HEARING MORE FROM THIS DONNIE SNOW BASTARD?
I CAN'T IMAGINE WE WILL--
ZZZZAT
--HE'S NOT REALLY E.L.E. MATERIAL.
I'M A GOOD GUY.
CRACK

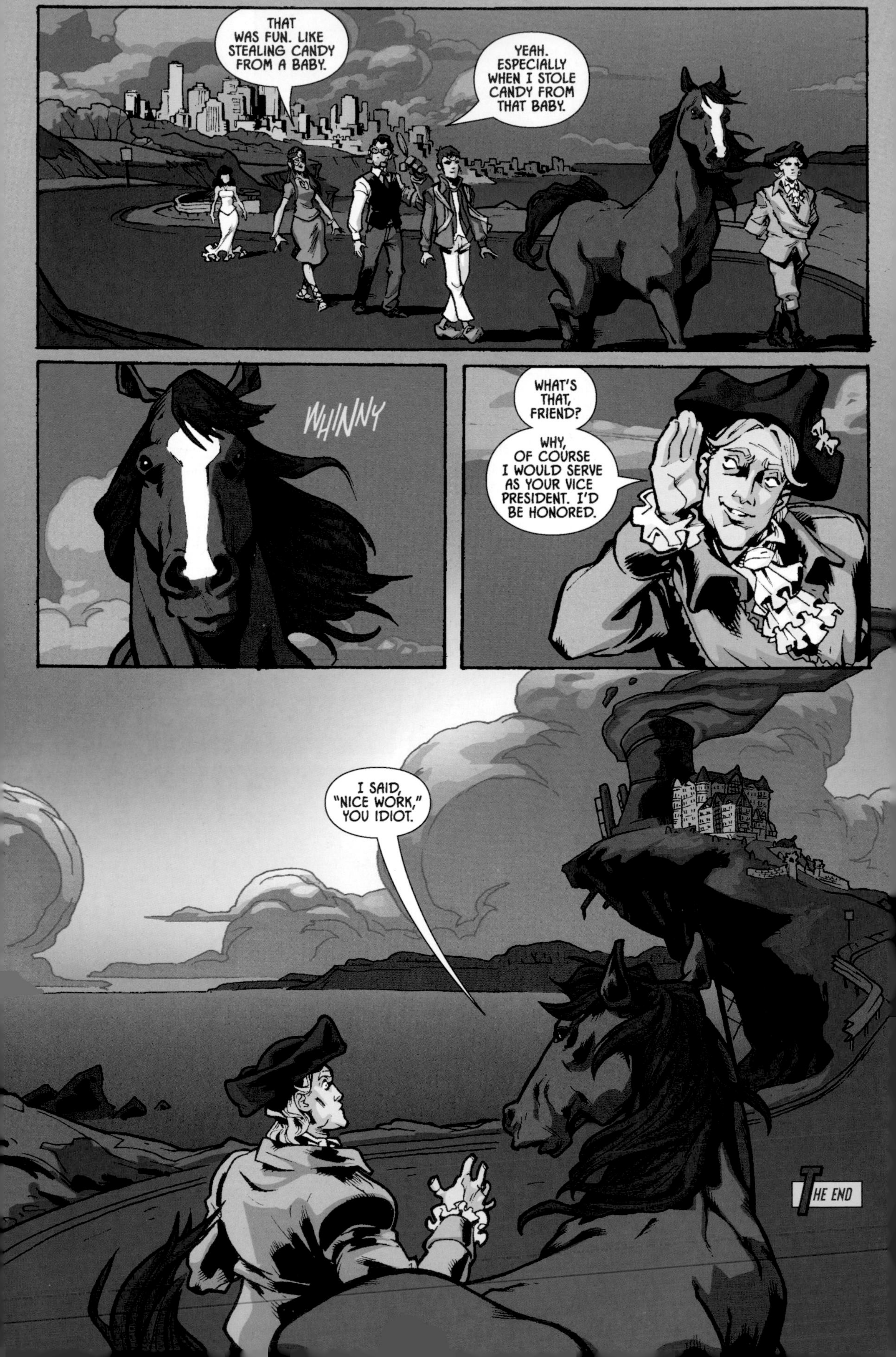
THAT WAS FUN. LIKE STEALING CANDY FROM A BABY.
YEAH. ESPECIALLY WHEN I STOLE CANDY FROM THAT BABY.
WHINNY
WHAT'S THAT, FRIEND?
WHY, OF COURSE I WOULD SERVE AS YOUR VICE PRESIDENT. I'D BE HONORED.
I SAID, "NICE WORK," YOU IDIOT.
THE END

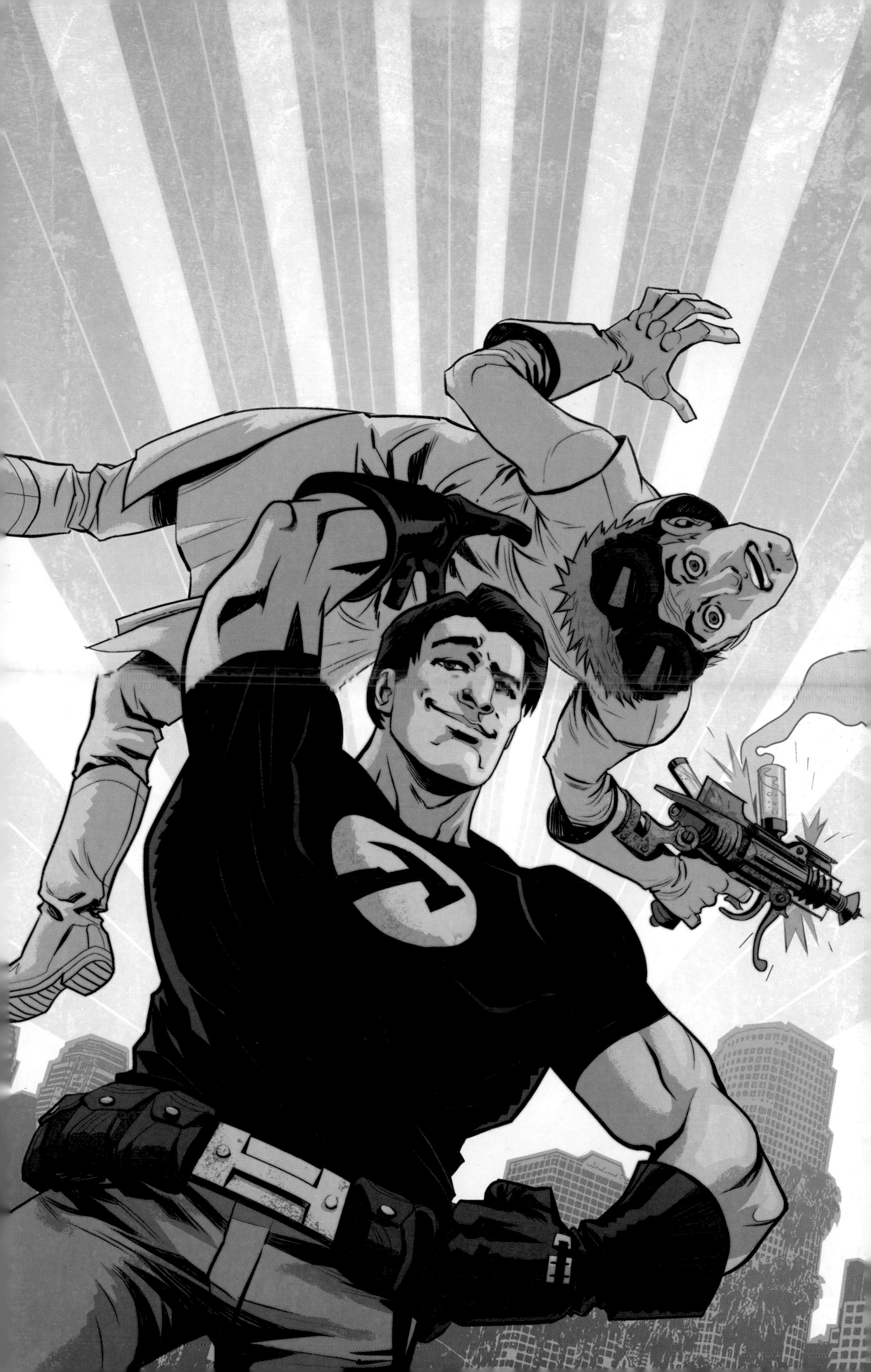

DR. HORRIBLE

Story by
ZACK WHEDON

Art by
JOËLLE JONES

Colors by
DAN JACKSON

Letters by
NATE PIEKOS OF BLAMBOT®

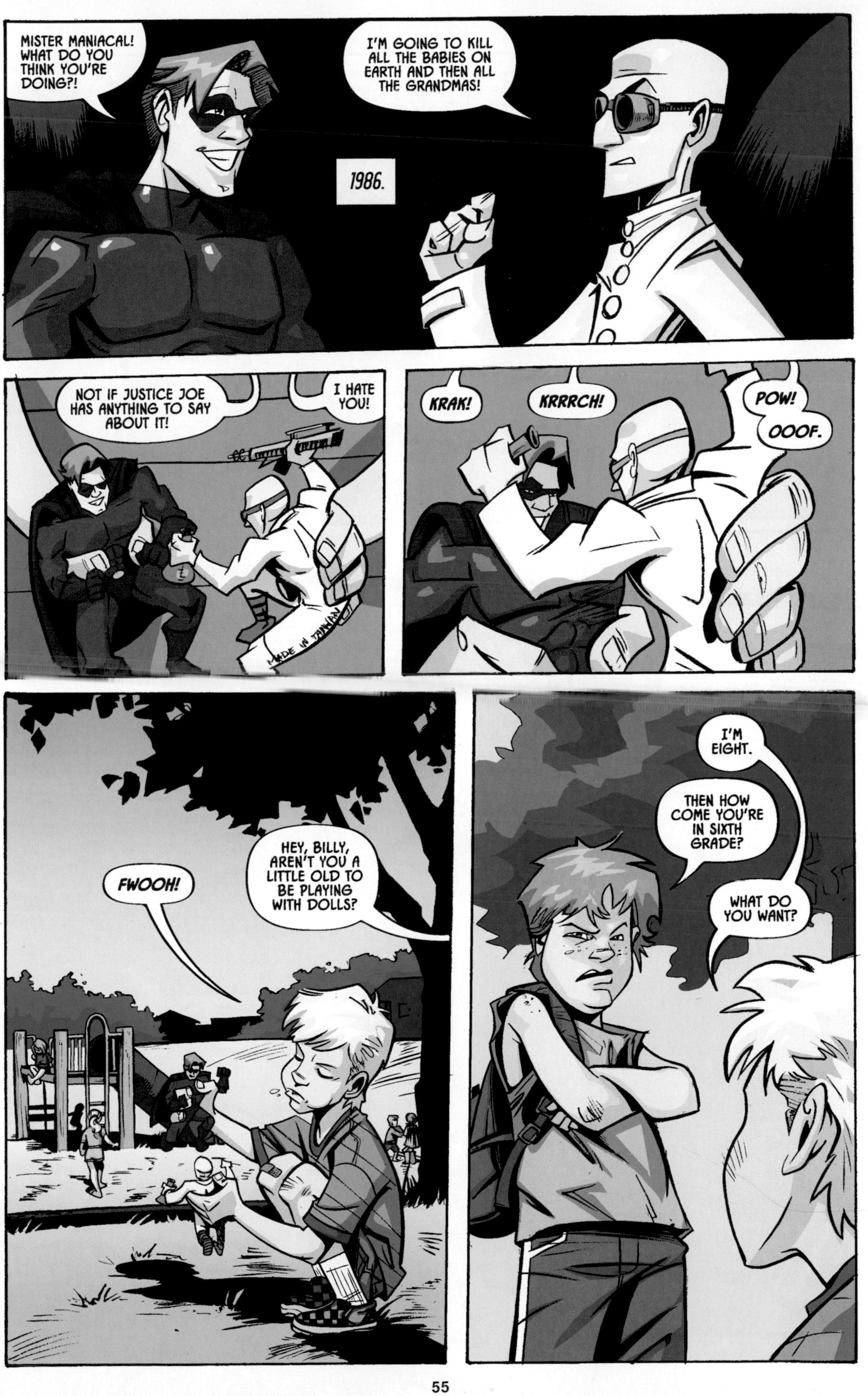
MISTER MANIACAL! WHAT DO YOU THINK YOU'RE DOING?!
I'M GOING TO KILL ALL THE BABIES ON EARTH AND THEN ALL THE GRANDMAS!
1986.
NOT IF JUSTICE JOE HAS ANYTHING TO SAY ABOUT IT!
I HATE YOU!
MADE IN TAIWAN
KRAK!
KRRRCH!
POW!
OOOF.
FWOOH!
HEY, BILLY, AREN'T YOU A LITTLE OLD TO BE PLAYING WITH DOLLS?
I'M EIGHT.
THEN HOW COME YOU'RE IN SIXTH GRADE?
WHAT DO YOU WANT?

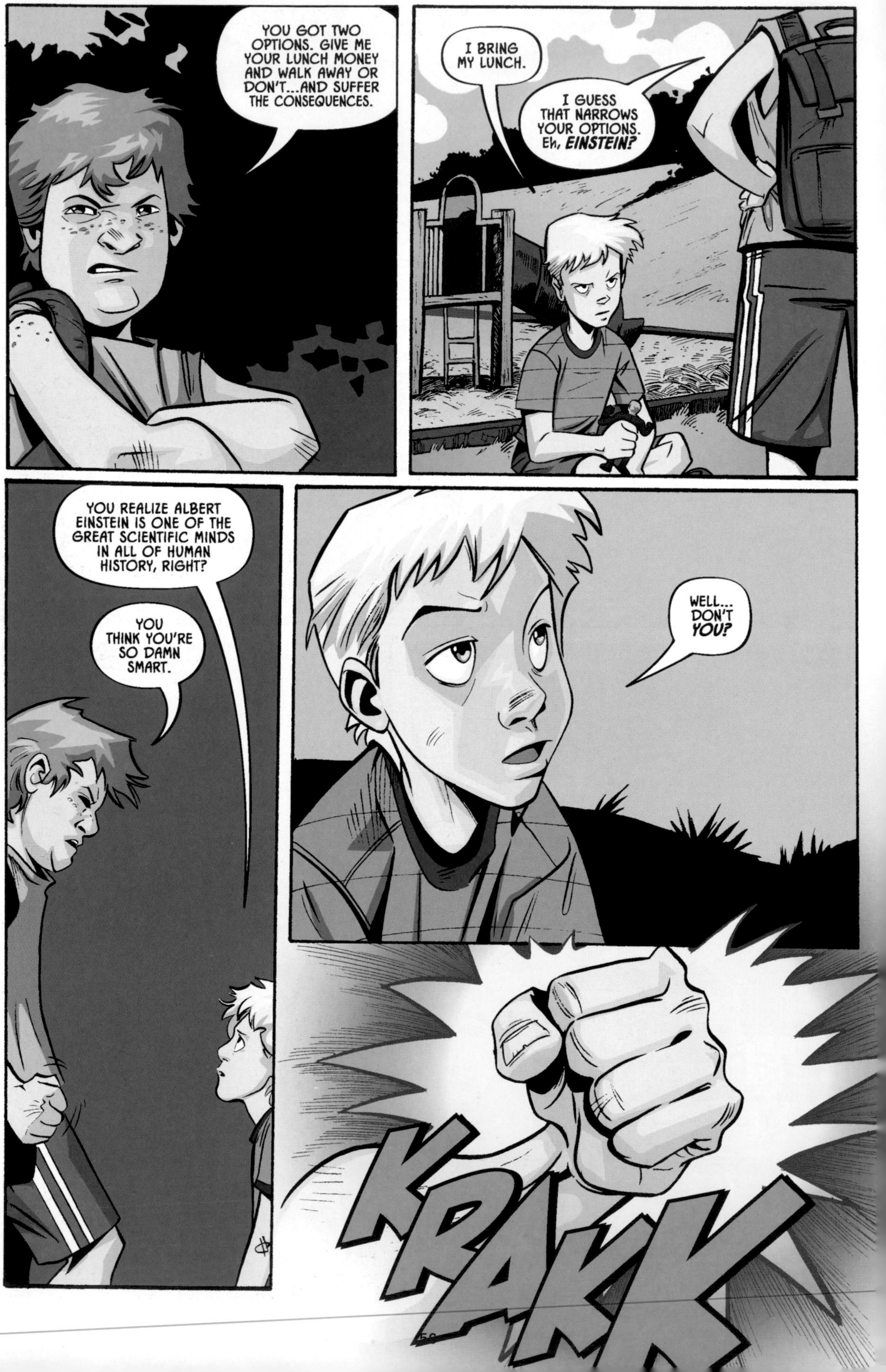
YOU GOT TWO OPTIONS. GIVE ME YOUR LUNCH MONEY AND WALK AWAY OR DON'T...AND SUFFER THE CONSEQUENCES.
I BRING MY LUNCH.
I GUESS THAT NARROWS YOUR OPTIONS. Eh, *EINSTEIN?*
YOU REALIZE ALBERT EINSTEIN IS ONE OF THE GREAT SCIENTIFIC MINDS IN ALL OF HUMAN HISTORY, RIGHT?
YOU THINK YOU'RE SO DAMN SMART.
WELL... DON'T *YOU?*
KRAKK

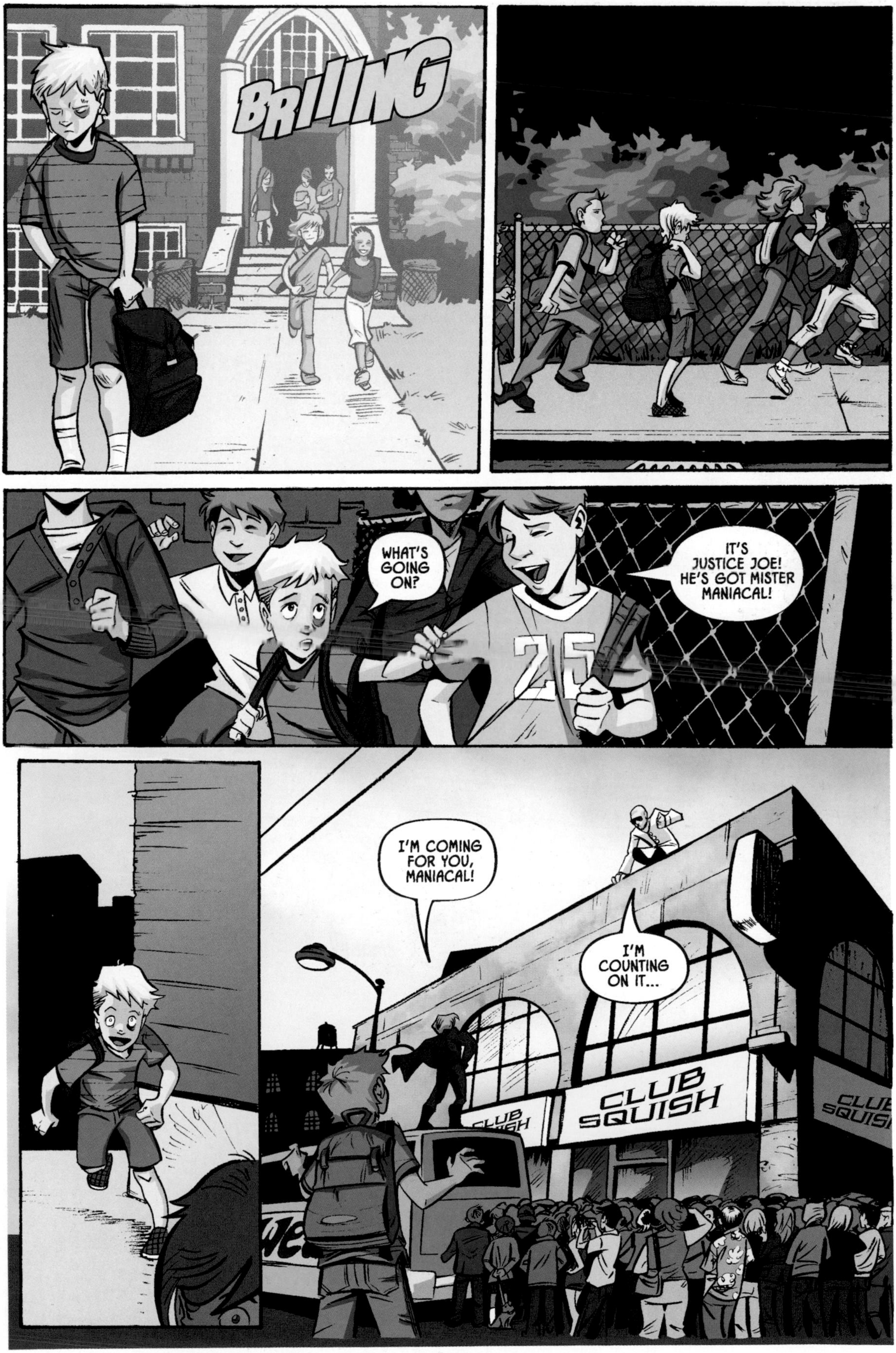
BRIIING
WHAT'S GOING ON?
IT'S JUSTICE JOE! HE'S GOT MISTER MANIACAL!
I'M COMING FOR YOU, MANIACAL!
I'M COUNTING ON IT...
CLUB SQUISH
CLUB SQUISH
CLUB SQUISH

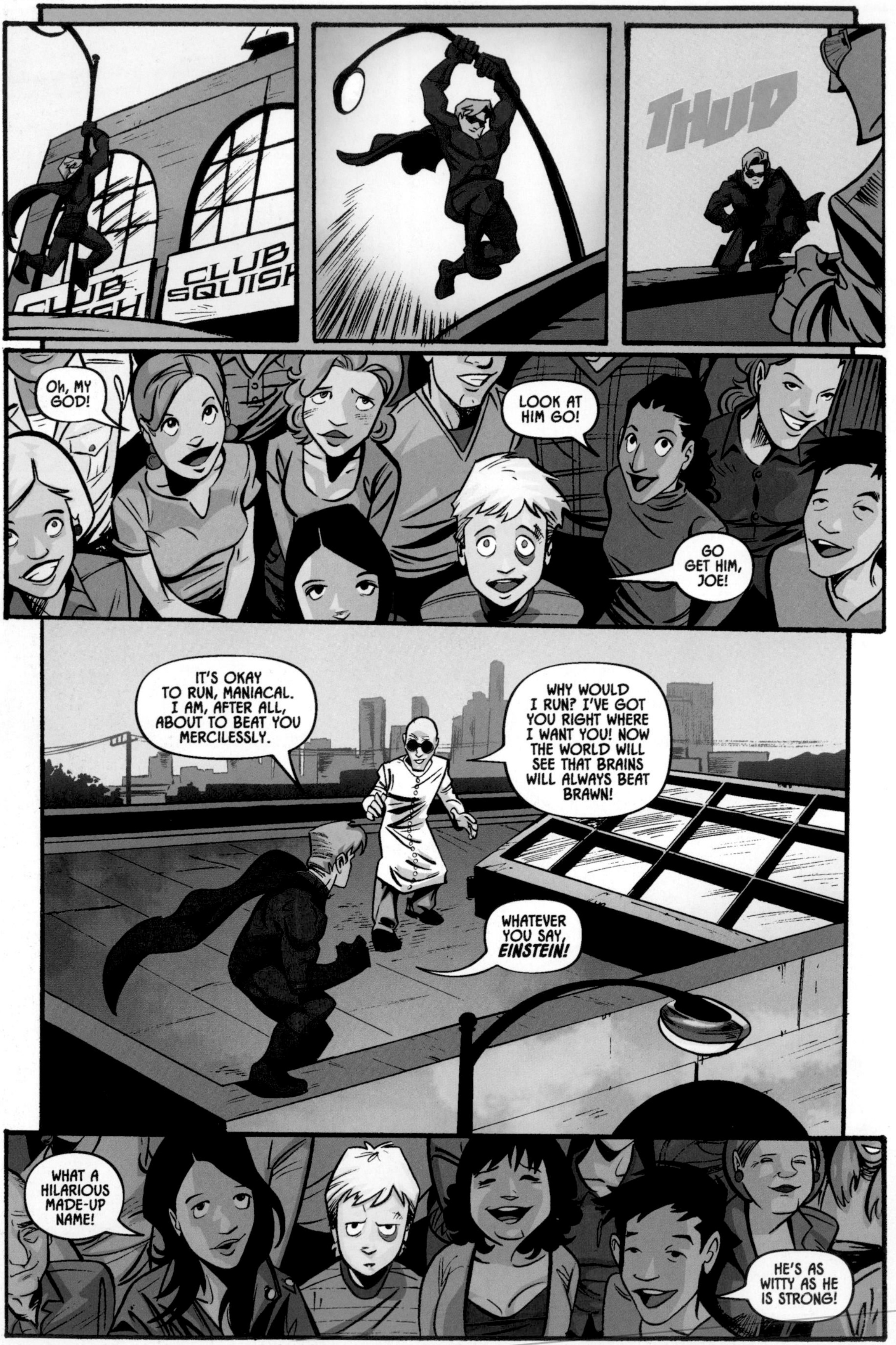
CLUB SQUISH
CLUB SQUISH
THUD
Oh, MY GOD!
LOOK AT HIM GO!
GO GET HIM, JOE!
IT'S OKAY TO RUN, MANIACAL. I AM, AFTER ALL, ABOUT TO BEAT YOU MERCILESSLY.
WHY WOULD I RUN? I'VE GOT YOU RIGHT WHERE I WANT YOU! NOW THE WORLD WILL SEE THAT BRAINS WILL ALWAYS BEAT BRAWN!
WHATEVER YOU SAY, *EINSTEIN!*
WHAT A HILARIOUS MADE-UP NAME!
HE'S AS WITTY AS HE IS STRONG!

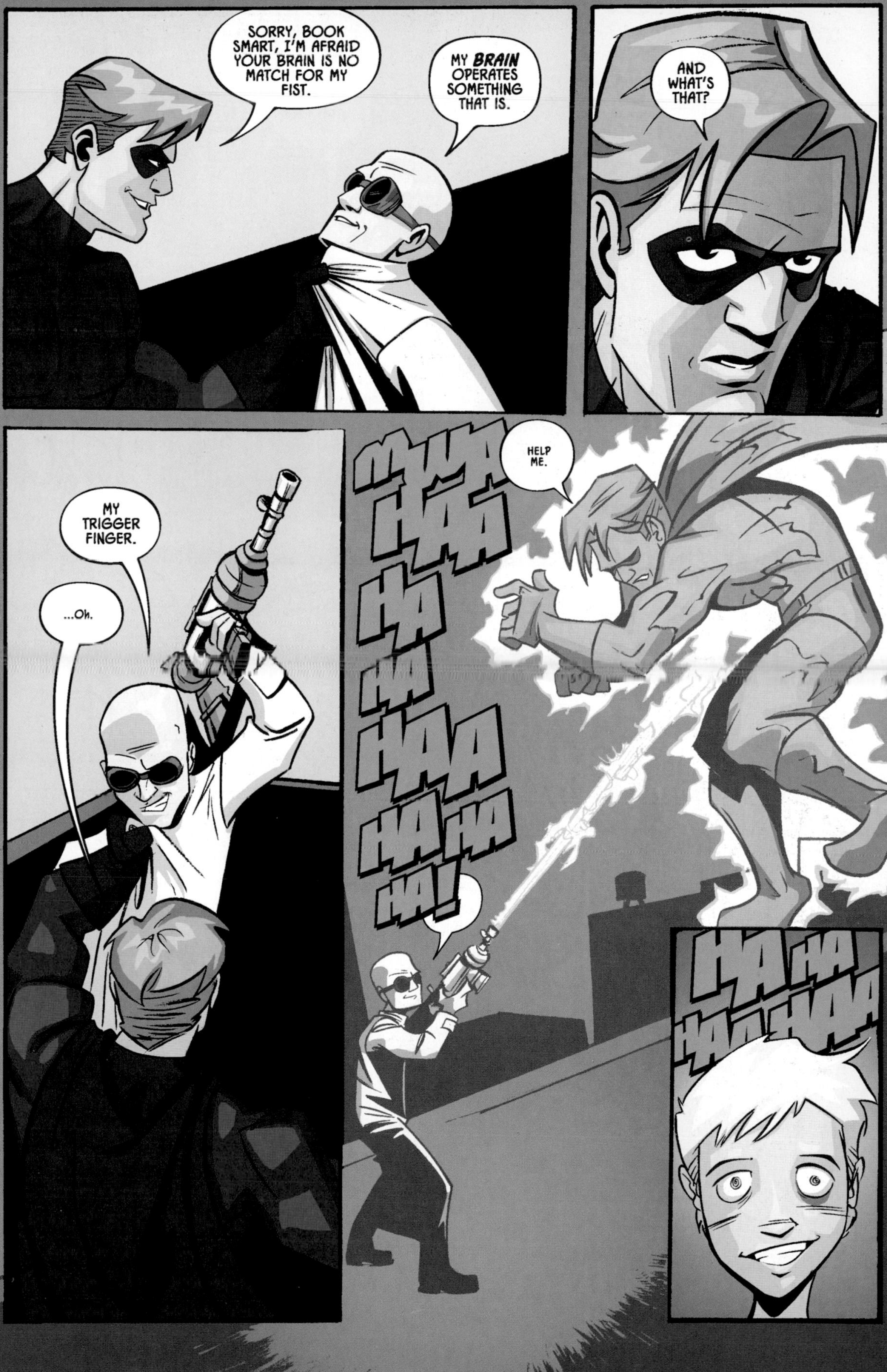
SORRY, BOOK SMART, I'M AFRAID YOUR BRAIN IS NO MATCH FOR MY FIST.
MY BRAIN OPERATES SOMETHING THAT IS.
AND WHAT'S THAT?
MY TRIGGER FINGER.
...Oh.
MWA HAA HA HA HAA HA HA HA!
HELP ME.
HA HA HAA HAA

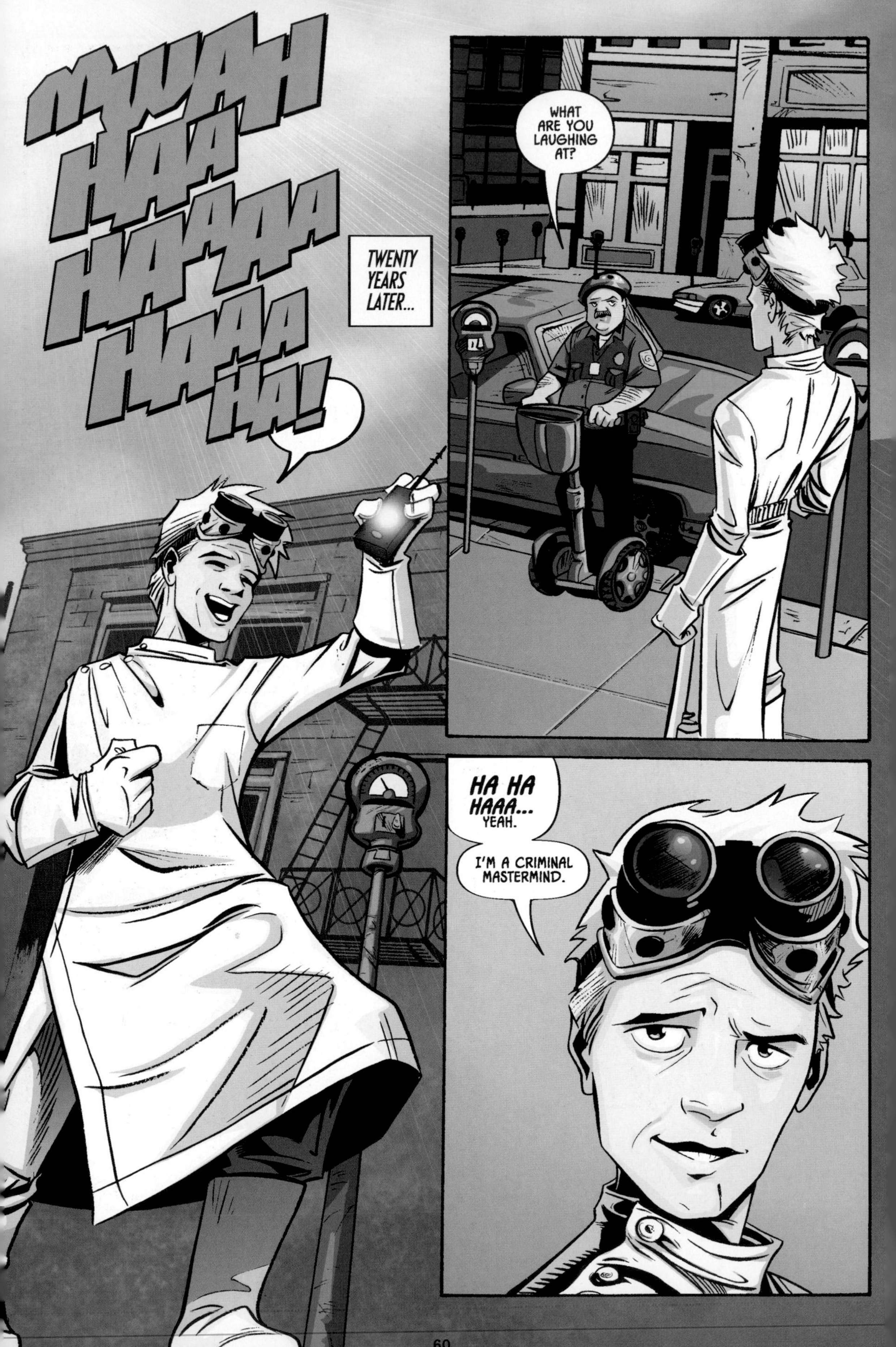
MWAH HAA HAAAA HAAA HA!
TWENTY YEARS LATER...
WHAT ARE YOU LAUGHING AT?
HA HA HAAA... YEAH.
I'M A CRIMINAL MASTERMIND.

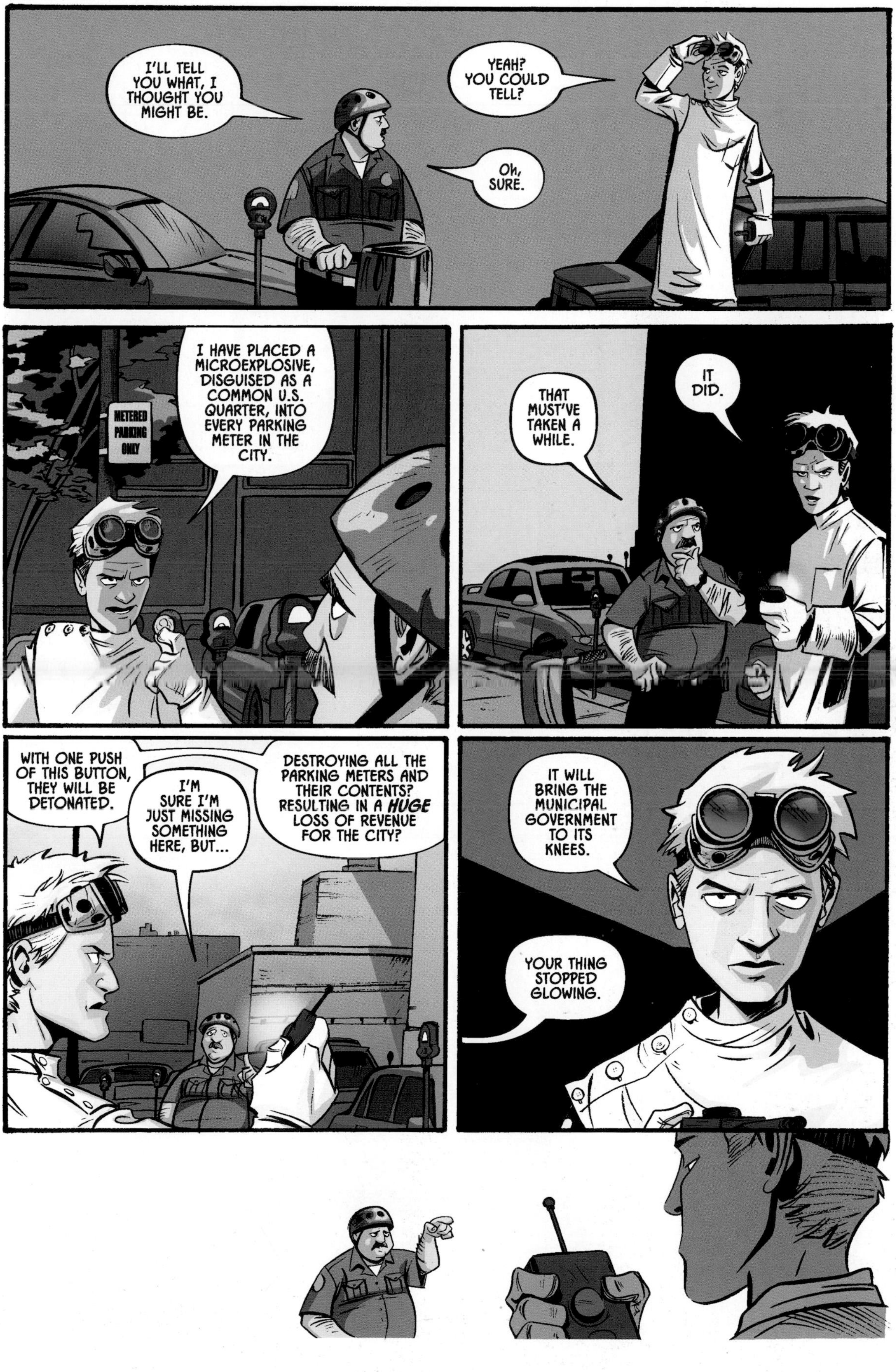

I'LL TELL YOU WHAT, I THOUGHT YOU MIGHT BE.
YEAH? YOU COULD TELL?
Oh, SURE.
METERED PARKING ONLY
I HAVE PLACED A MICROEXPLOSIVE, DISGUISED AS A COMMON U.S. QUARTER, INTO EVERY PARKING METER IN THE CITY.
THAT MUST'VE TAKEN A WHILE.
IT DID.
WITH ONE PUSH OF THIS BUTTON, THEY WILL BE DETONATED.
I'M SURE I'M JUST MISSING SOMETHING HERE, BUT...
DESTROYING ALL THE PARKING METERS AND THEIR CONTENTS? RESULTING IN A *HUGE* LOSS OF REVENUE FOR THE CITY?
IT WILL BRING THE MUNICIPAL GOVERNMENT TO ITS KNEES.
YOUR THING STOPPED GLOWING.

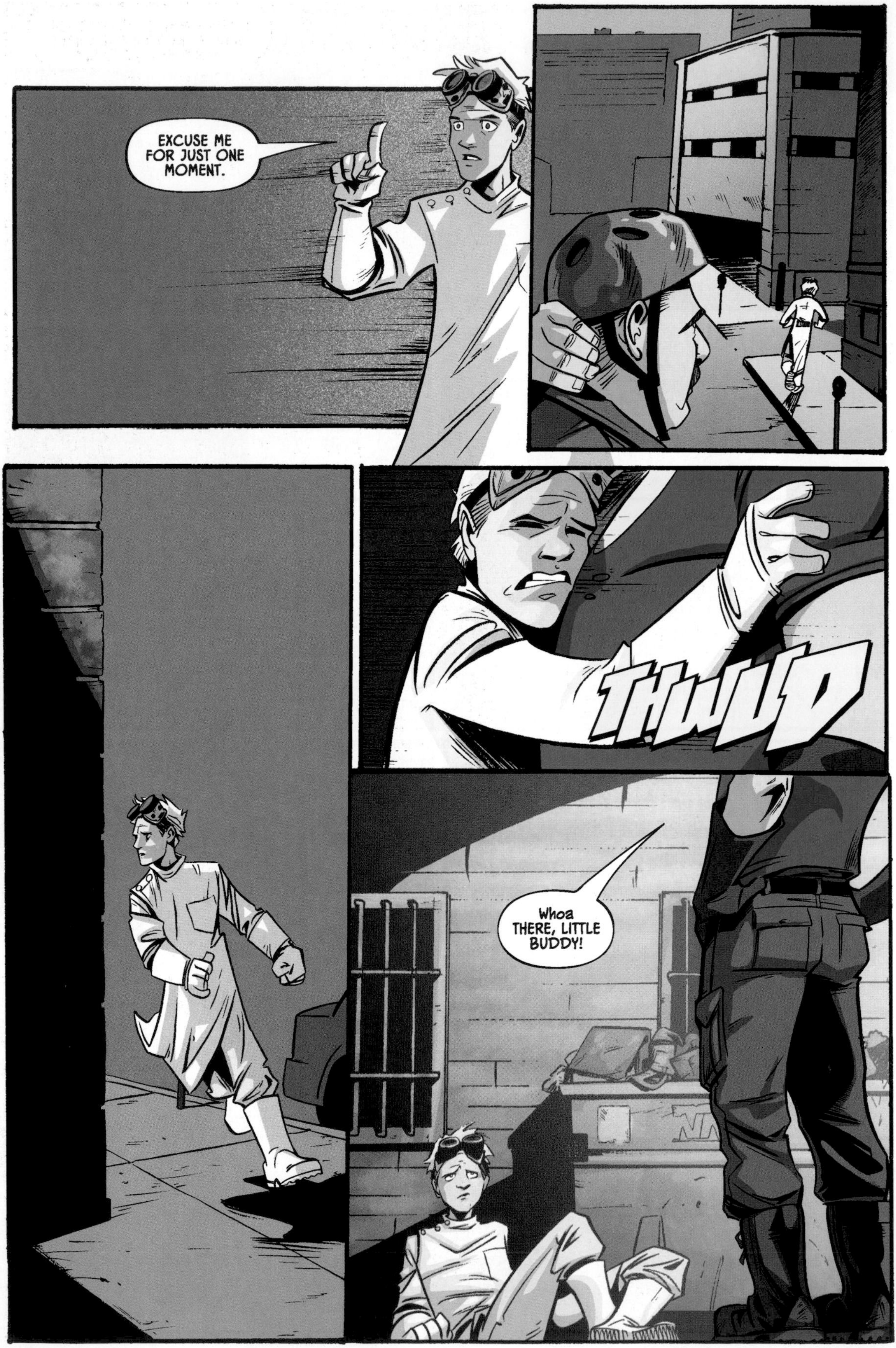
EXCUSE ME FOR JUST ONE MOMENT.
THWUD
Whoa THERE, LITTLE BUDDY!

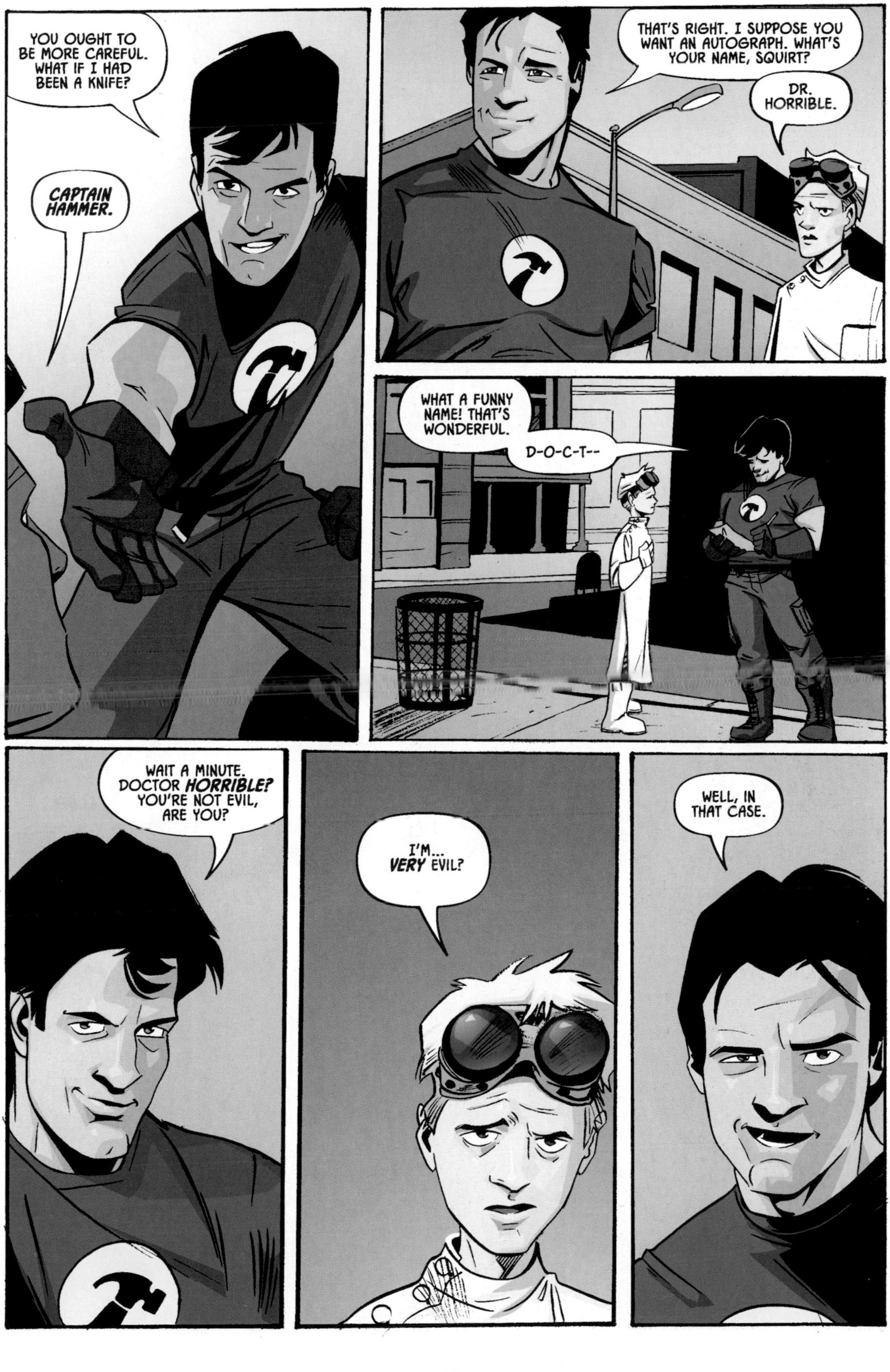
YOU OUGHT TO BE MORE CAREFUL. WHAT IF I HAD BEEN A KNIFE?
CAPTAIN HAMMER.
THAT'S RIGHT. I SUPPOSE YOU WANT AN AUTOGRAPH. WHAT'S YOUR NAME, SQUIRT?
DR. HORRIBLE.
WHAT A FUNNY NAME! THAT'S WONDERFUL.
D-O-C-T--
WAIT A MINUTE. DOCTOR HORRIBLE? YOU'RE NOT EVIL, ARE YOU?
I'M... VERY EVIL?
WELL, IN THAT CASE.

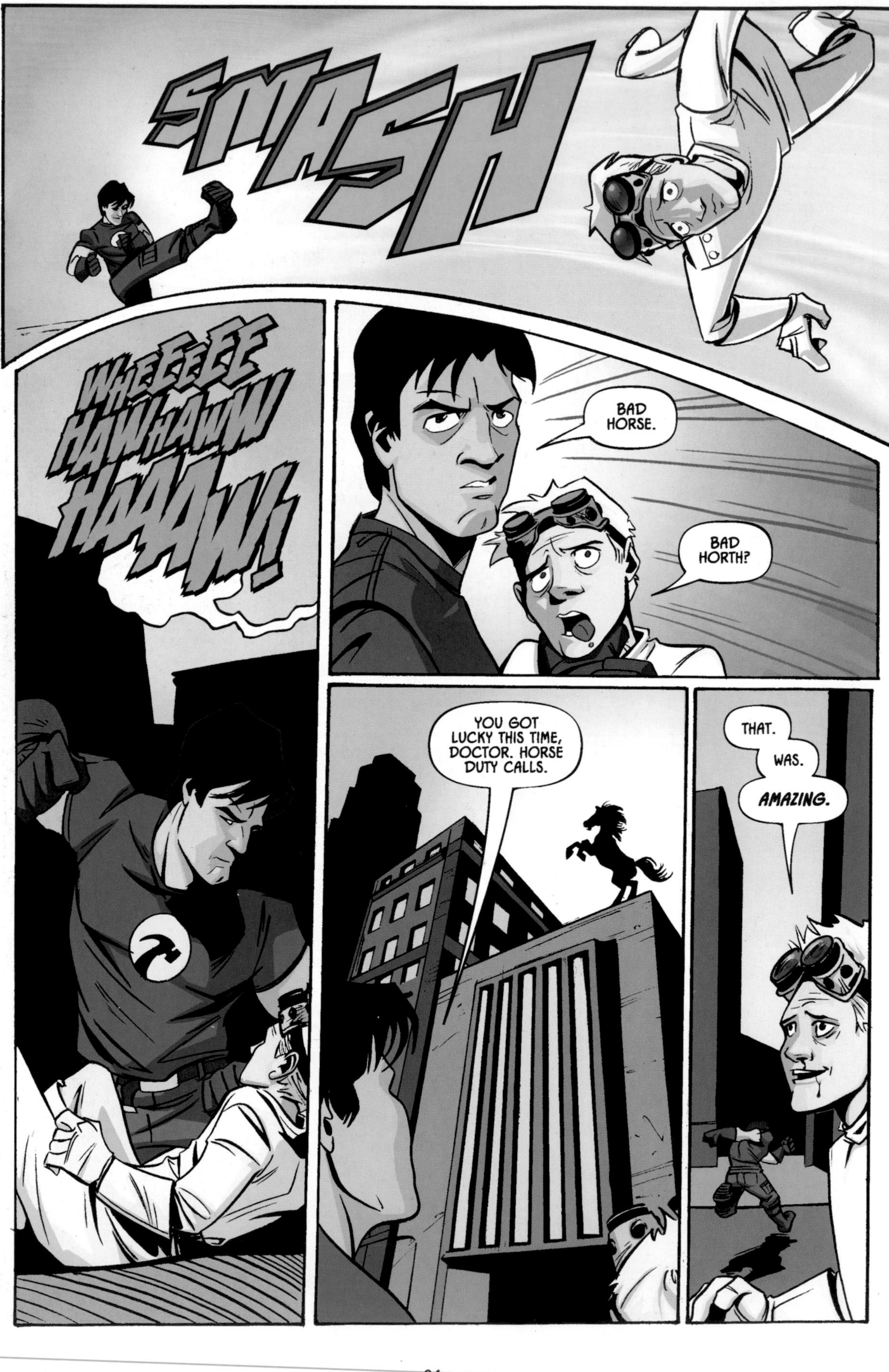
SMASH
WHEEEEE HAWHAWW HAAAW!
BAD HORSE.
BAD HORTH?
YOU GOT LUCKY THIS TIME, DOCTOR. HORSE DUTY CALLS.
THAT.
WAS.
AMAZING.

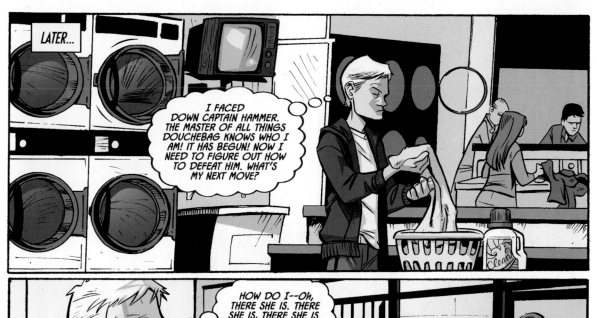

LATER...

I FACED DOWN CAPTAIN HAMMER. THE MASTER OF ALL THINGS DOUCHEBAG KNOWS WHO I AM! IT HAS BEGUN! NOW I NEED TO FIGURE OUT HOW TO DEFEAT HIM. WHAT'S MY NEXT MOVE?

HOW DO I--Oh, THERE SHE IS. THERE SHE IS, THERE SHE IS. DON'T PANIC. ACT NATURAL.

IS THIS HOW I USUALLY FOLD MY LAUNDRY? IT SEEMS FORCED ALL OF A SUDDEN.

OH!

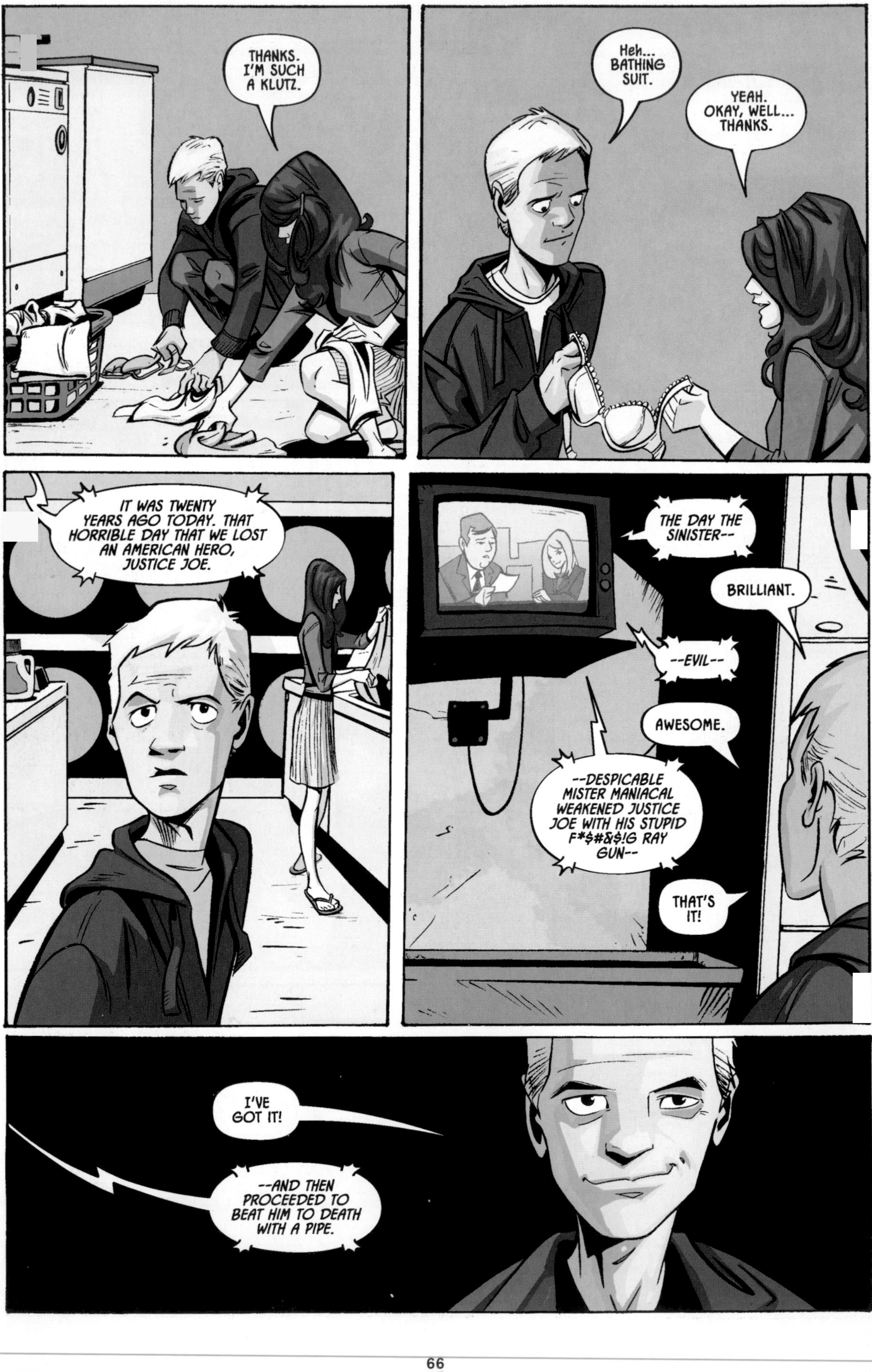
THANKS. I'M SUCH A KLUTZ.
Heh... BATHING SUIT.
YEAH. OKAY, WELL... THANKS.
IT WAS TWENTY YEARS AGO TODAY. THAT HORRIBLE DAY THAT WE LOST AN AMERICAN HERO, JUSTICE JOE.
THE DAY THE SINISTER--
BRILLIANT.
--EVIL--
AWESOME.
--DESPICABLE MISTER MANIACAL WEAKENED JUSTICE JOE WITH HIS STUPID F*$#&$!G RAY GUN--
THAT'S IT!
I'VE GOT IT!
--AND THEN PROCEEDED TO BEAT HIM TO DEATH WITH A PIPE.

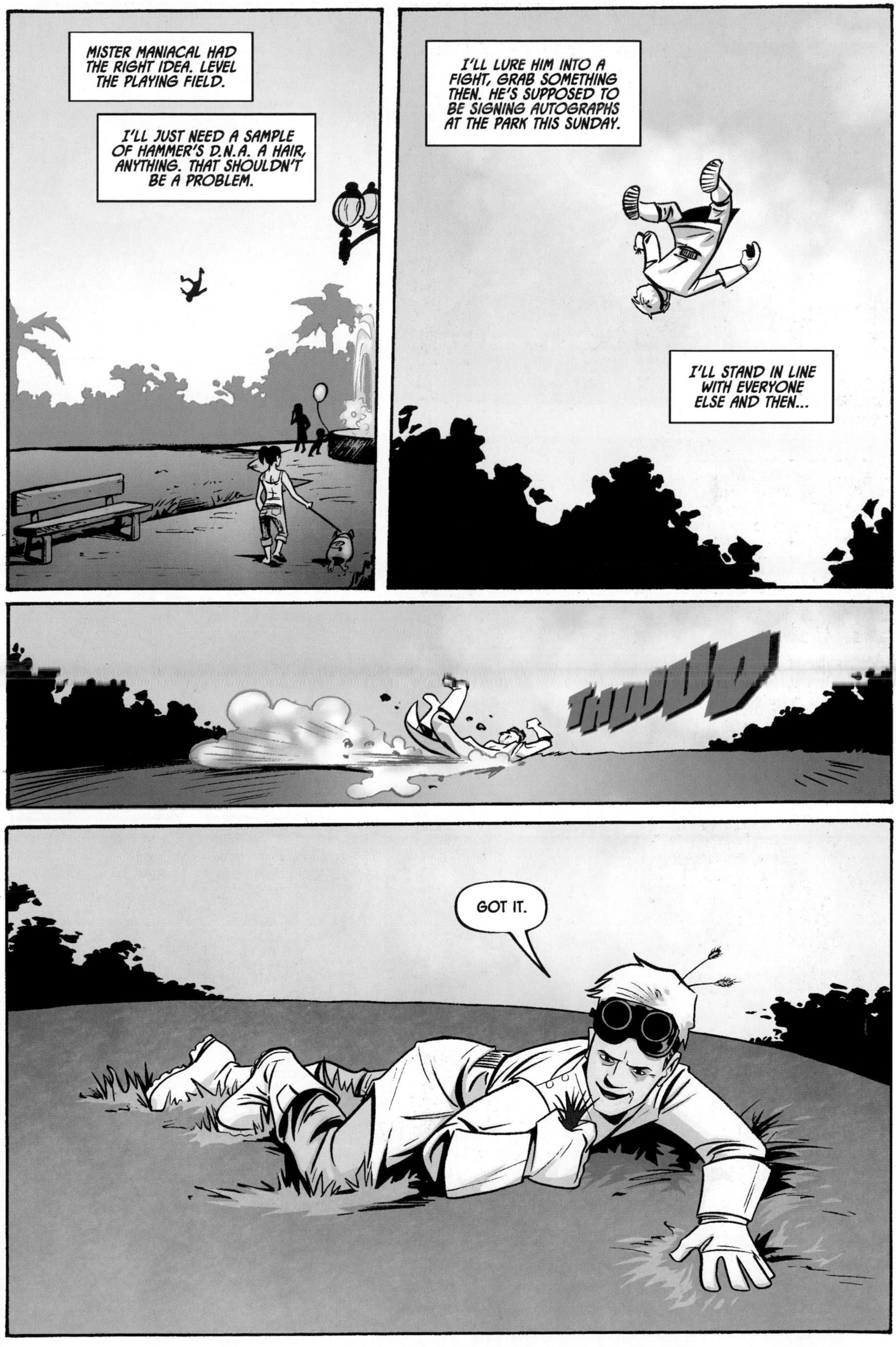
MISTER MANIACAL HAD THE RIGHT IDEA. LEVEL THE PLAYING FIELD.
I'LL JUST NEED A SAMPLE OF HAMMER'S D.N.A. A HAIR, ANYTHING. THAT SHOULDN'T BE A PROBLEM.
I'LL LURE HIM INTO A FIGHT, GRAB SOMETHING THEN. HE'S SUPPOSED TO BE SIGNING AUTOGRAPHS AT THE PARK THIS SUNDAY.
I'LL STAND IN LINE WITH EVERYONE ELSE AND THEN...
THUUD
GOT IT.

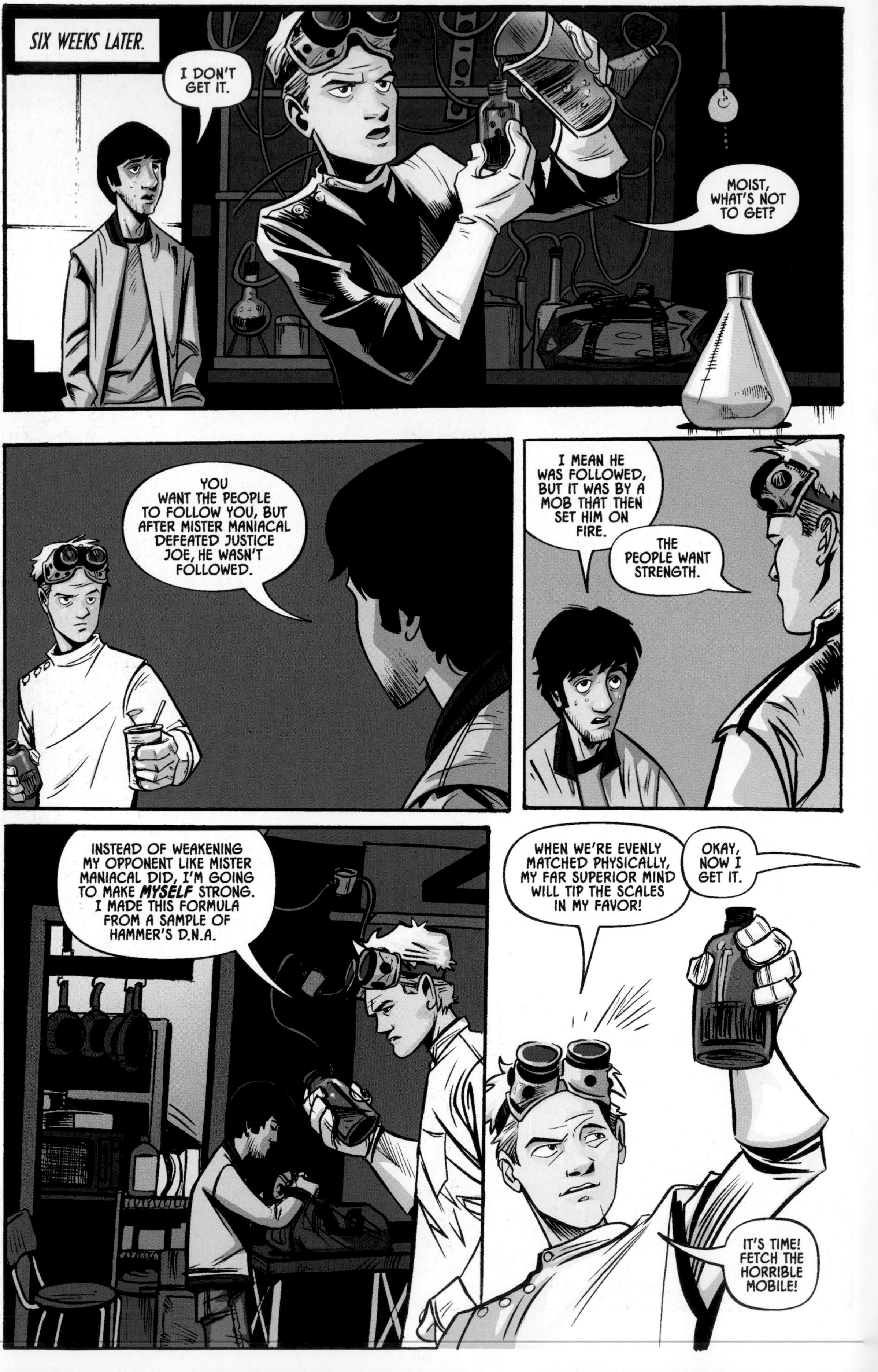
SIX WEEKS LATER.
I DON'T GET IT.
MOIST, WHAT'S NOT TO GET?
YOU WANT THE PEOPLE TO FOLLOW YOU, BUT AFTER MISTER MANIACAL DEFEATED JUSTICE JOE, HE WASN'T FOLLOWED.
I MEAN HE WAS FOLLOWED, BUT IT WAS BY A MOB THAT THEN SET HIM ON FIRE.
THE PEOPLE WANT STRENGTH.
INSTEAD OF WEAKENING MY OPPONENT LIKE MISTER MANIACAL DID, I'M GOING TO MAKE MYSELF STRONG. I MADE THIS FORMULA FROM A SAMPLE OF HAMMER'S D.N.A.
WHEN WE'RE EVENLY MATCHED PHYSICALLY, MY FAR SUPERIOR MIND WILL TIP THE SCALES IN MY FAVOR!
OKAY, NOW I GET IT.
IT'S TIME! FETCH THE HORRIBLE MOBILE!

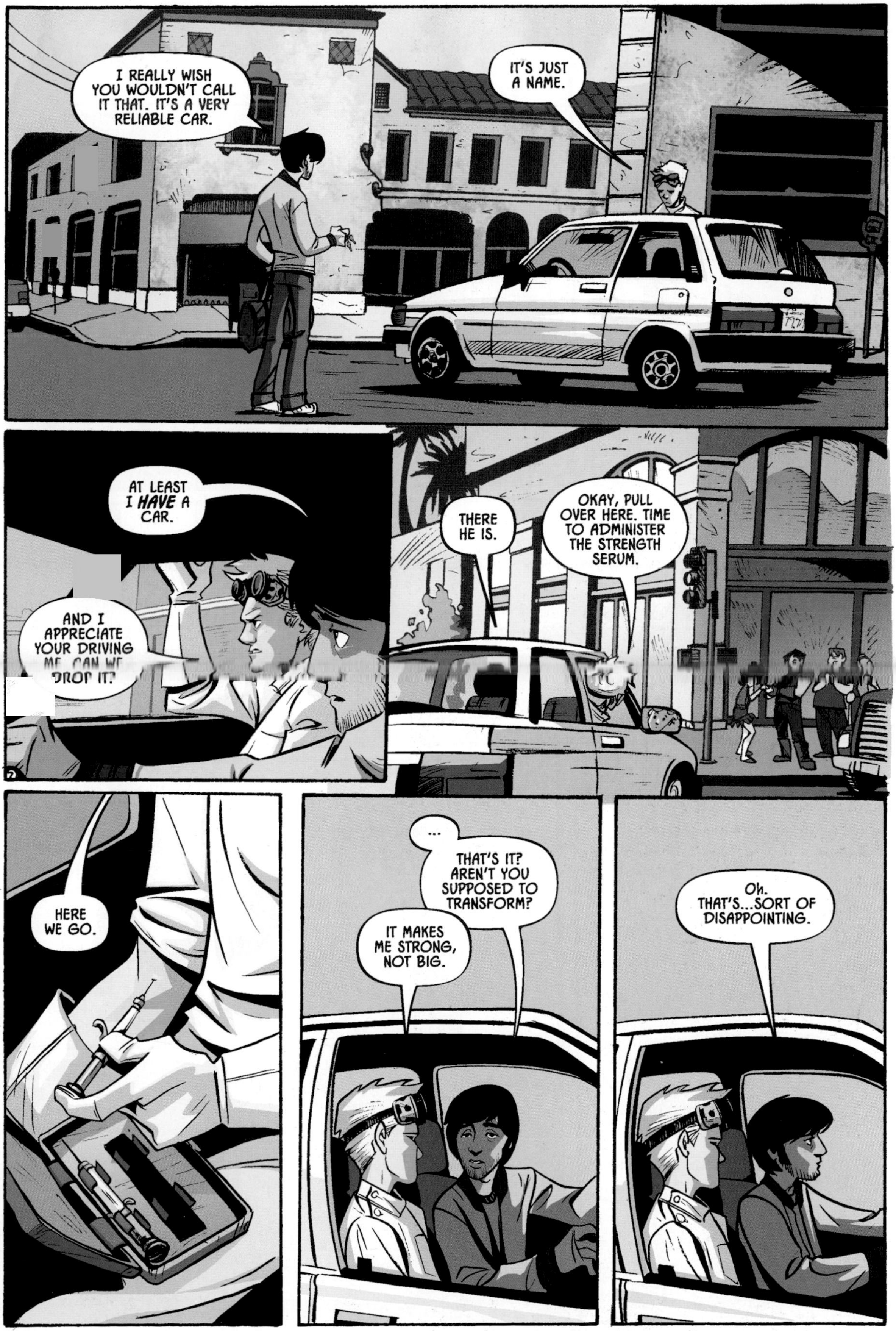

I REALLY WISH YOU WOULDN'T CALL IT THAT. IT'S A VERY RELIABLE CAR.
IT'S JUST A NAME.
AT LEAST I ***HAVE*** A CAR.
AND I APPRECIATE YOUR DRIVING ME. CAN WE DROP IT?
THERE HE IS.
OKAY, PULL OVER HERE. TIME TO ADMINISTER THE STRENGTH SERUM.
HERE WE GO.
...
THAT'S IT? AREN'T YOU SUPPOSED TO TRANSFORM?
IT MAKES ME STRONG, NOT BIG.
Oh. THAT'S...SORT OF DISAPPOINTING.

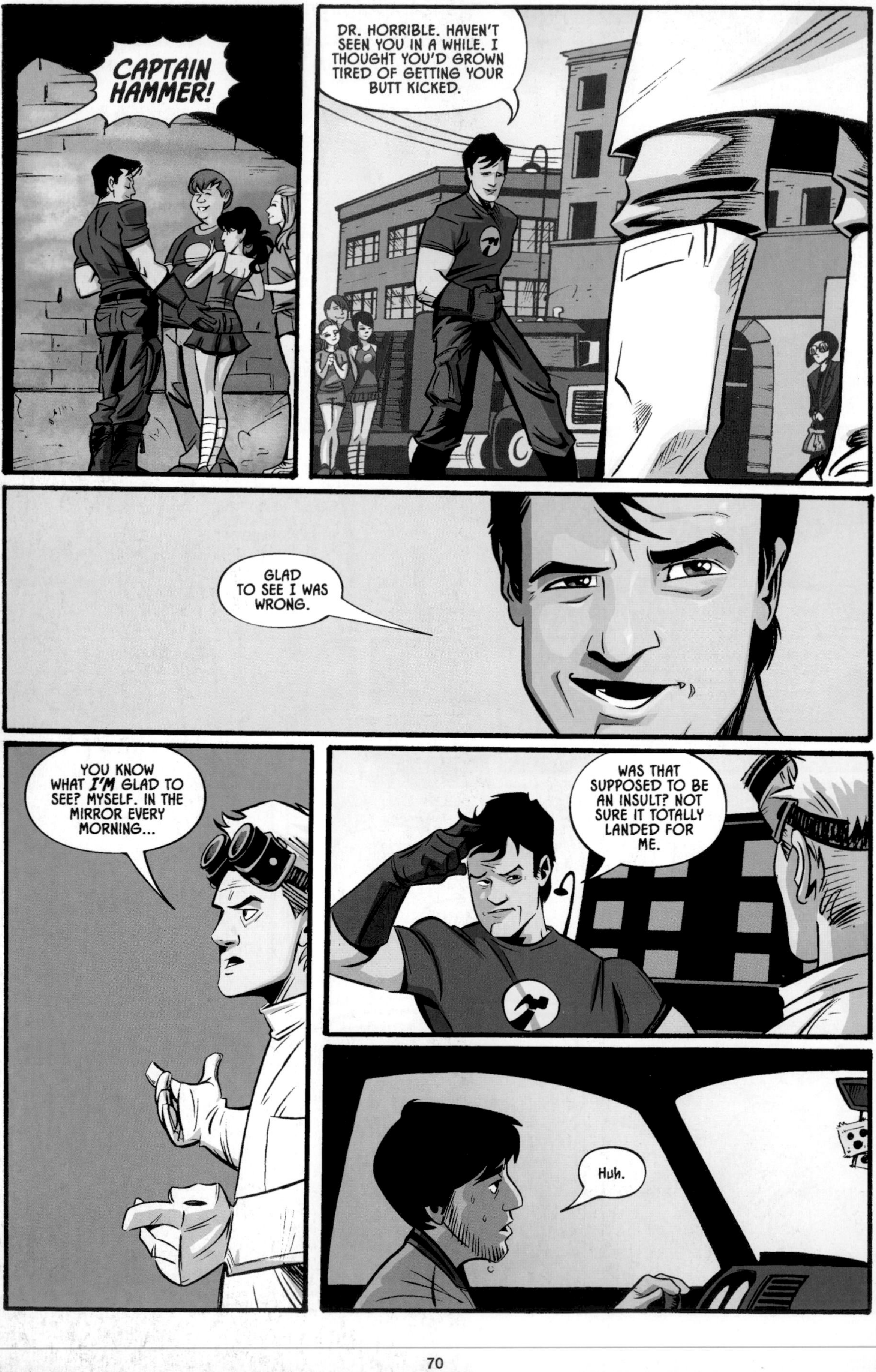
CAPTAIN HAMMER!
DR. HORRIBLE. HAVEN'T SEEN YOU IN A WHILE. I THOUGHT YOU'D GROWN TIRED OF GETTING YOUR BUTT KICKED.
GLAD TO SEE I WAS WRONG.
YOU KNOW WHAT *I'M* GLAD TO SEE? MYSELF. IN THE MIRROR EVERY MORNING...
WAS THAT SUPPOSED TO BE AN INSULT? NOT SURE IT TOTALLY LANDED FOR ME.
Huh.

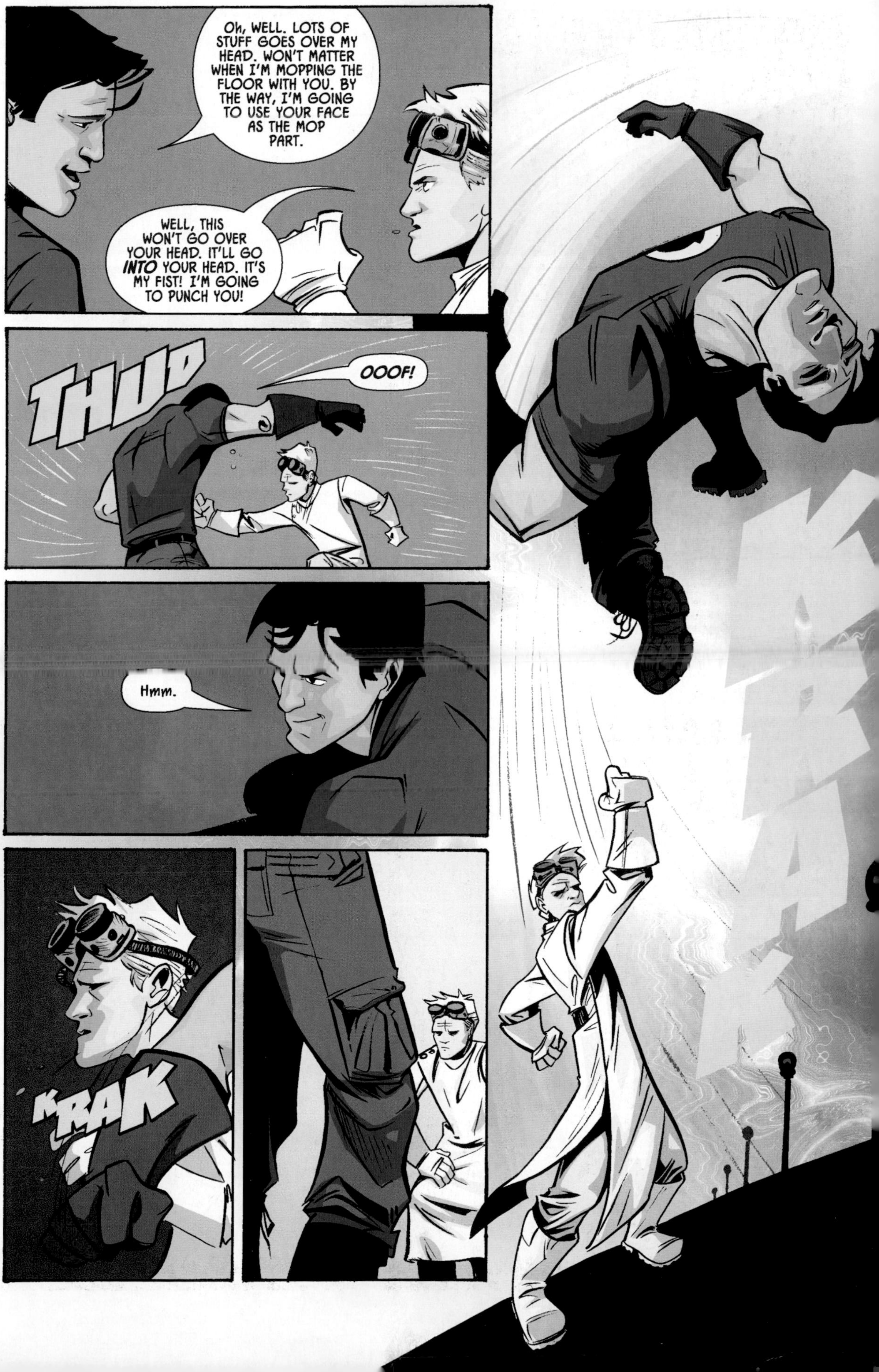
Oh, WELL. LOTS OF STUFF GOES OVER MY HEAD. WON'T MATTER WHEN I'M MOPPING THE FLOOR WITH YOU. BY THE WAY, I'M GOING TO USE YOUR FACE AS THE MOP PART.
WELL, THIS WON'T GO OVER YOUR HEAD. IT'LL GO INTO YOUR HEAD. IT'S MY FIST! I'M GOING TO PUNCH YOU!
THUD
OOOF!
Hmm.
KRAK

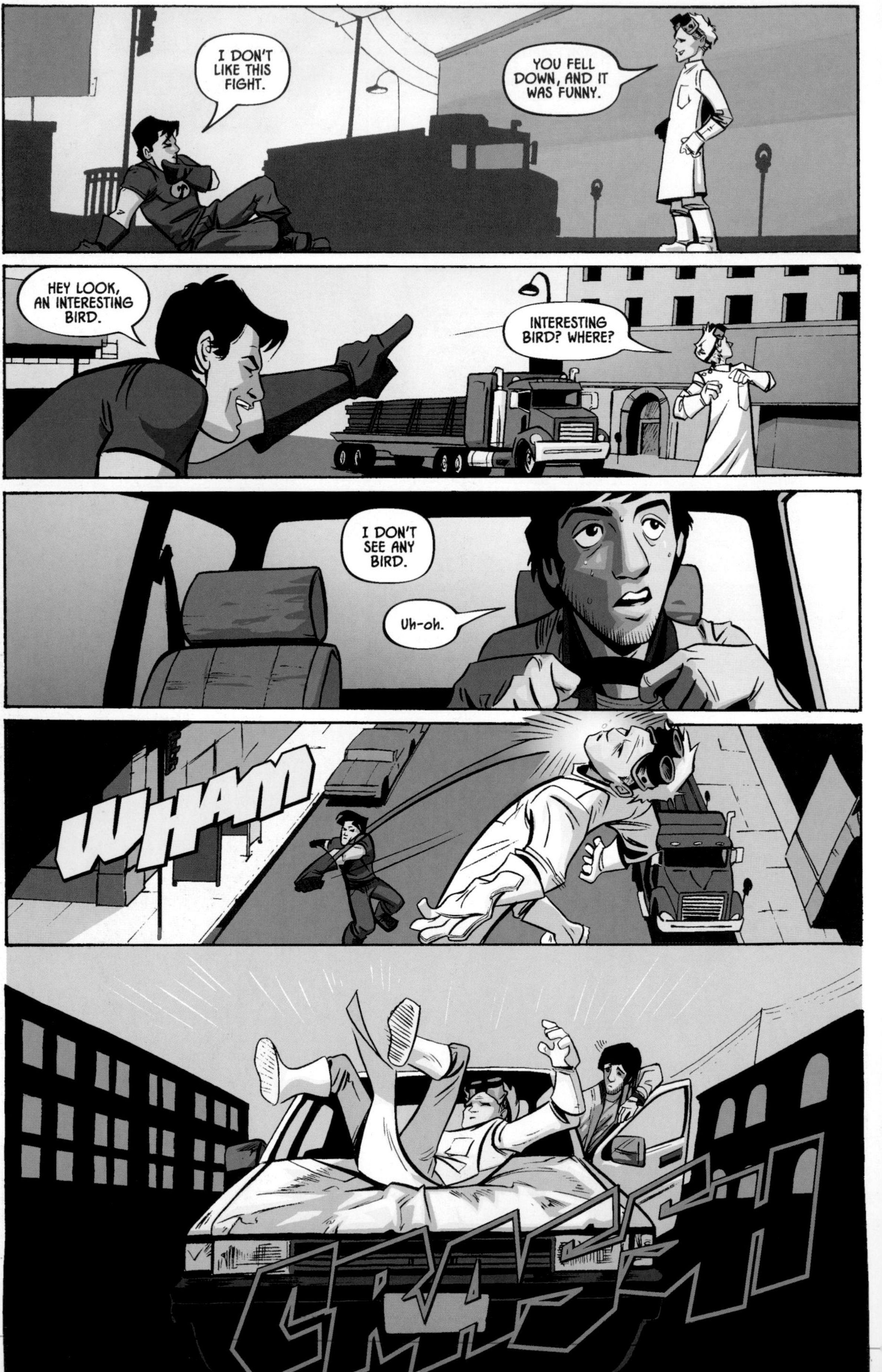
I DON'T LIKE THIS FIGHT.
YOU FELL DOWN, AND IT WAS FUNNY.
HEY LOOK, AN INTERESTING BIRD.
INTERESTING BIRD? WHERE?
I DON'T SEE ANY BIRD.
Uh-oh.
WHAM
CRASH

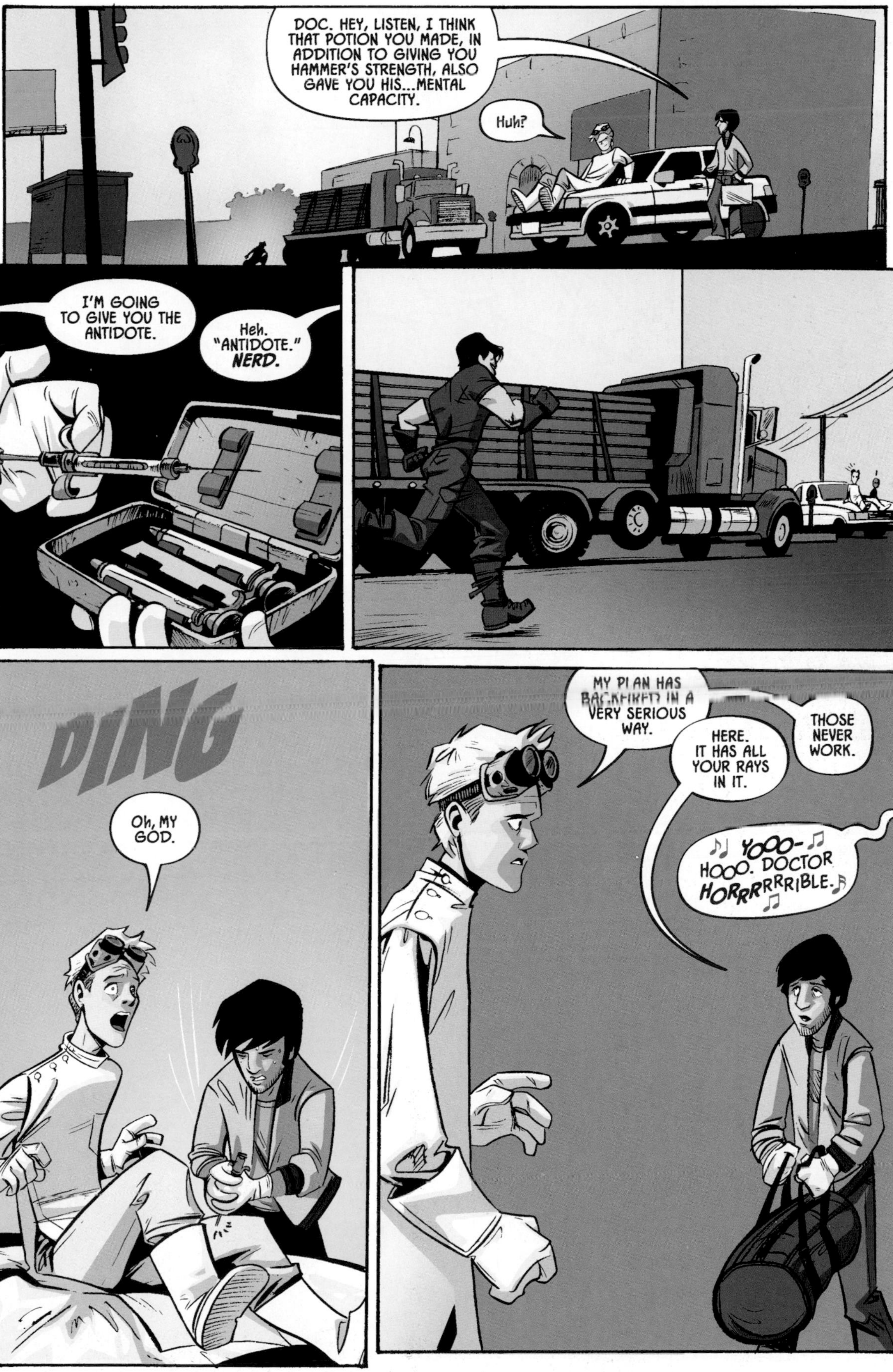
DOC. HEY, LISTEN, I THINK THAT POTION YOU MADE, IN ADDITION TO GIVING YOU HAMMER'S STRENGTH, ALSO GAVE YOU HIS...MENTAL CAPACITY.
Huh?
I'M GOING TO GIVE YOU THE ANTIDOTE.
Heh. "ANTIDOTE." NERD.
DING
Oh, MY GOD.
MY PLAN HAS BACKFIRED IN A VERY SERIOUS WAY.
HERE. IT HAS ALL YOUR RAYS IN IT.
THOSE NEVER WORK.
YOOO-HOOO. DOCTOR HORRRRRRIBLE.

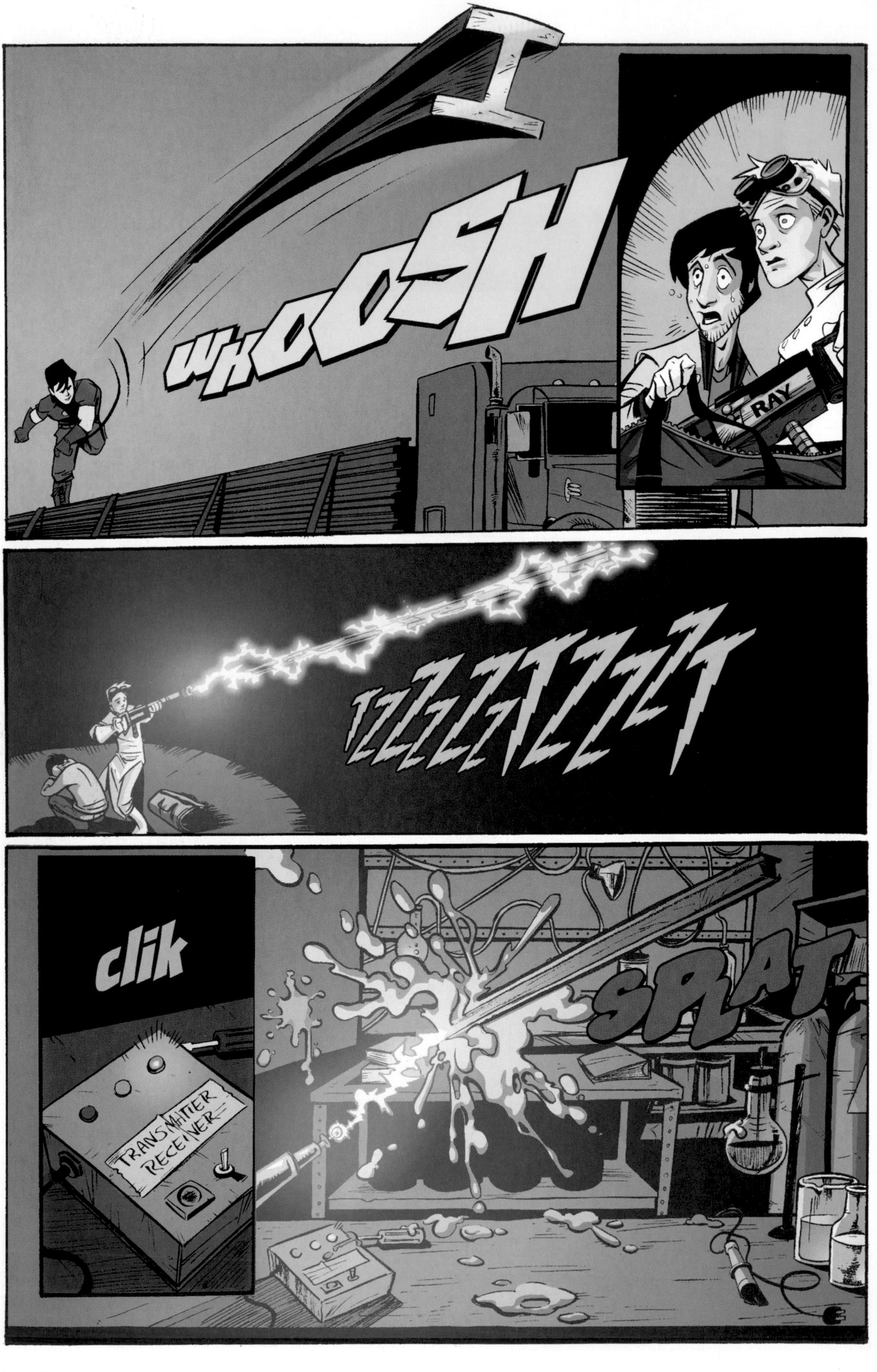
WHOOSH
RAY
TZZZZZZZZZ
clik
TRANSMATTIER RECEIVER
SPLAT

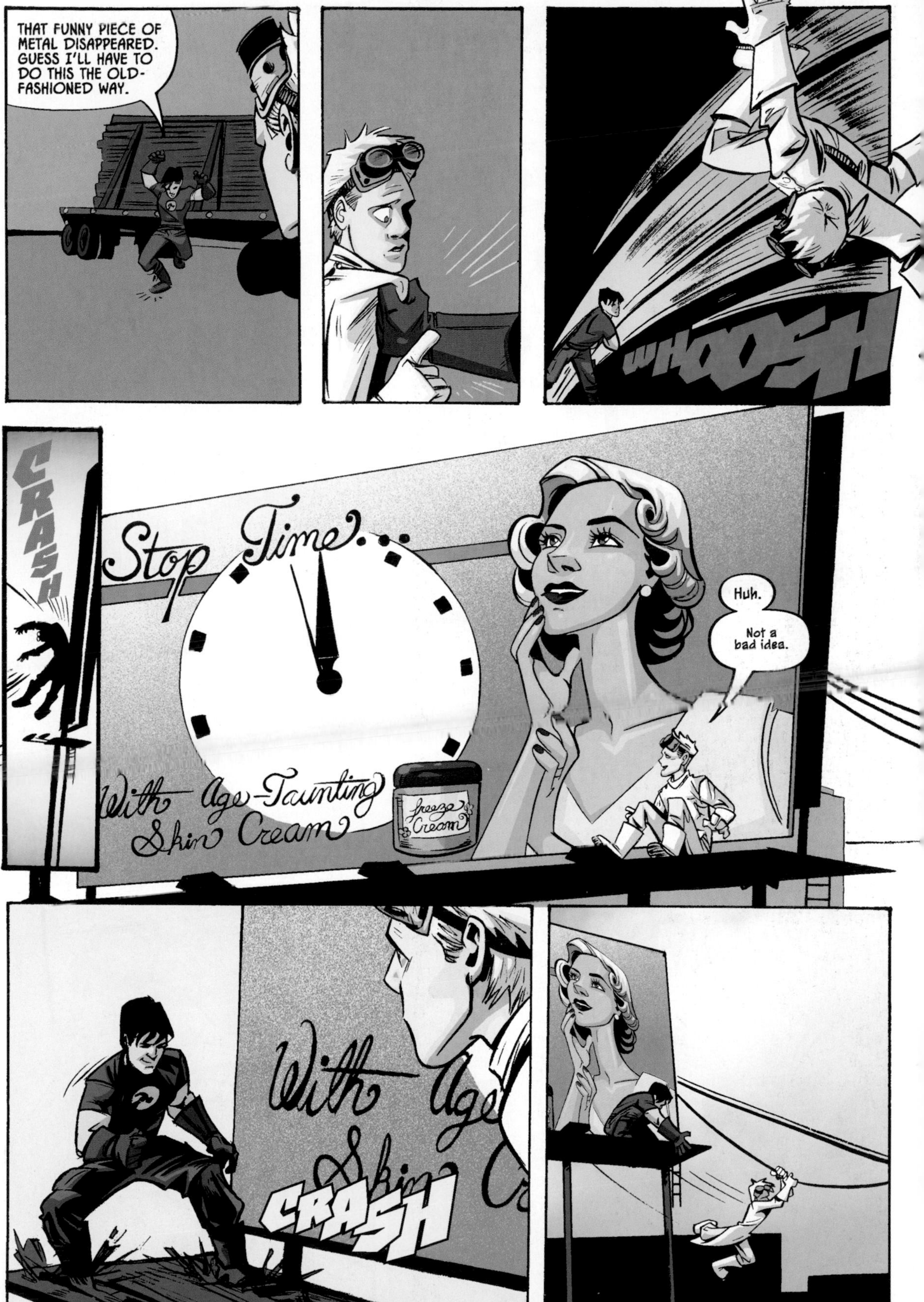
THAT FUNNY PIECE OF METAL DISAPPEARED. GUESS I'LL HAVE TO DO THIS THE OLD-FASHIONED WAY.
WHOOSH
CRASH
Stop Time...
With Age-Taunting Skin Cream
freeze Cream
Huh.
Not a bad idea.
With Age
Skin C
CRASH

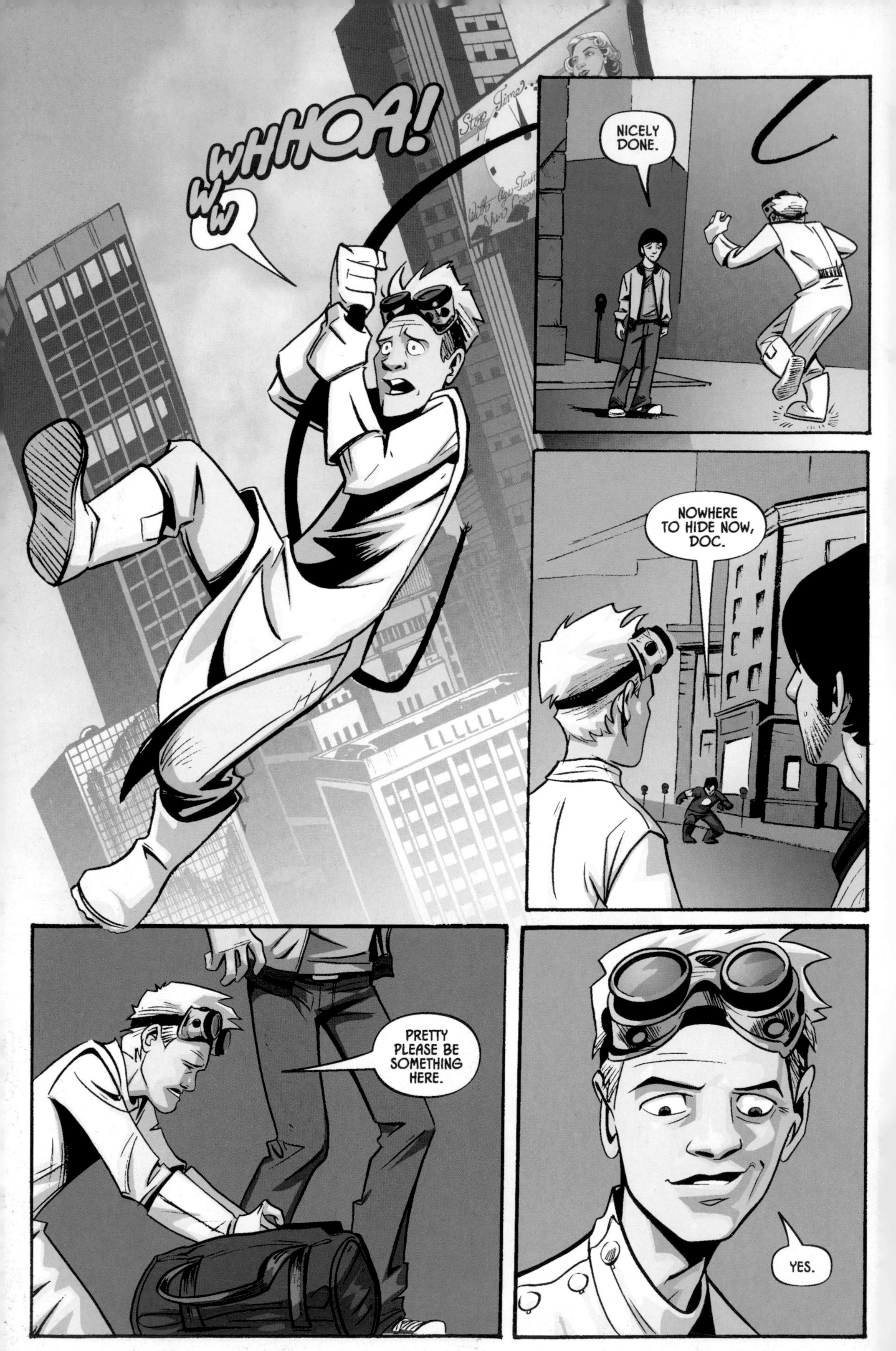
WWWHHOA!
NICELY DONE.
NOWHERE TO HIDE NOW, DOC.
PRETTY PLEASE BE SOMETHING HERE.
YES.

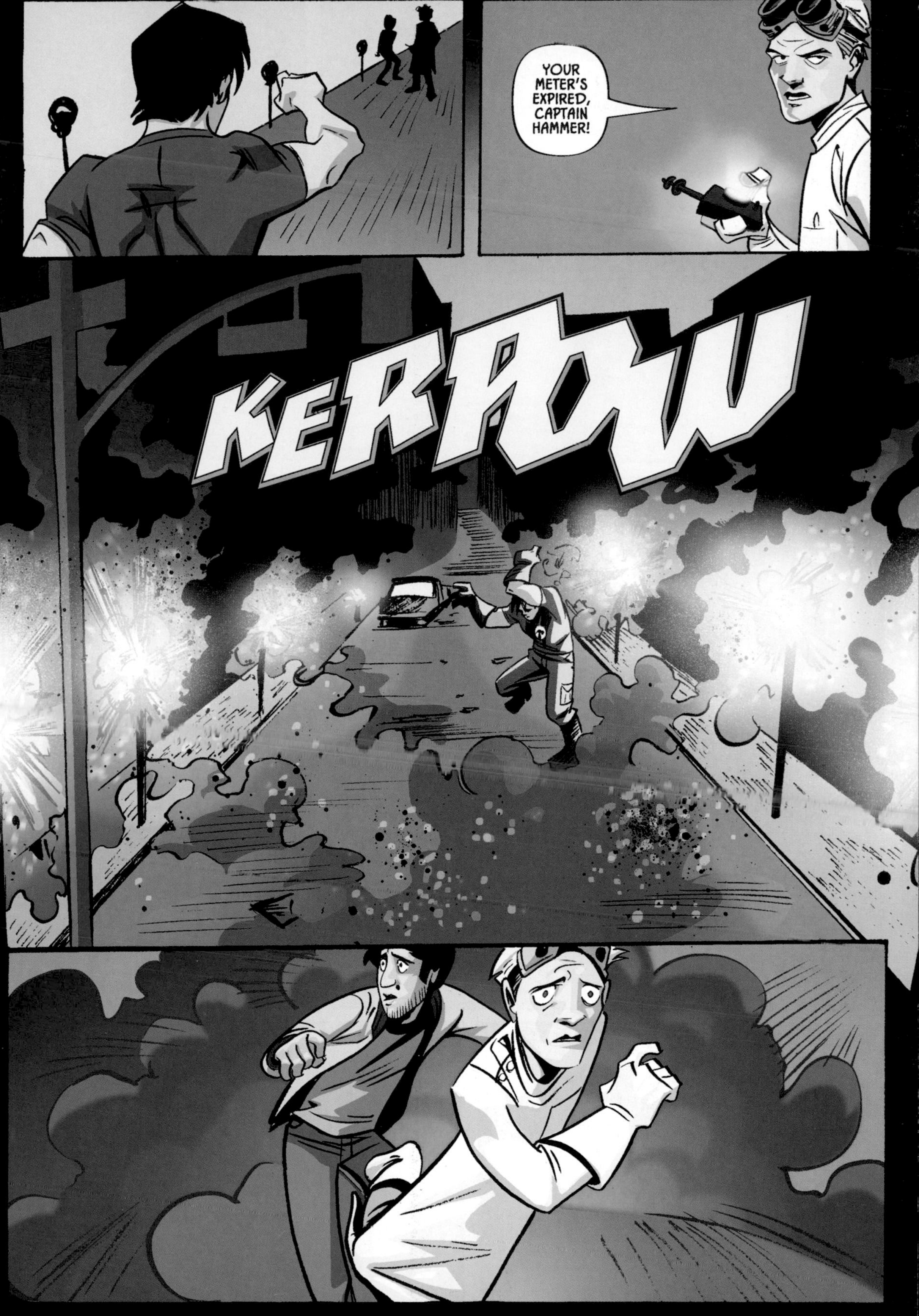
YOUR METER'S EXPIRED, CAPTAIN HAMMER!
KERPOW

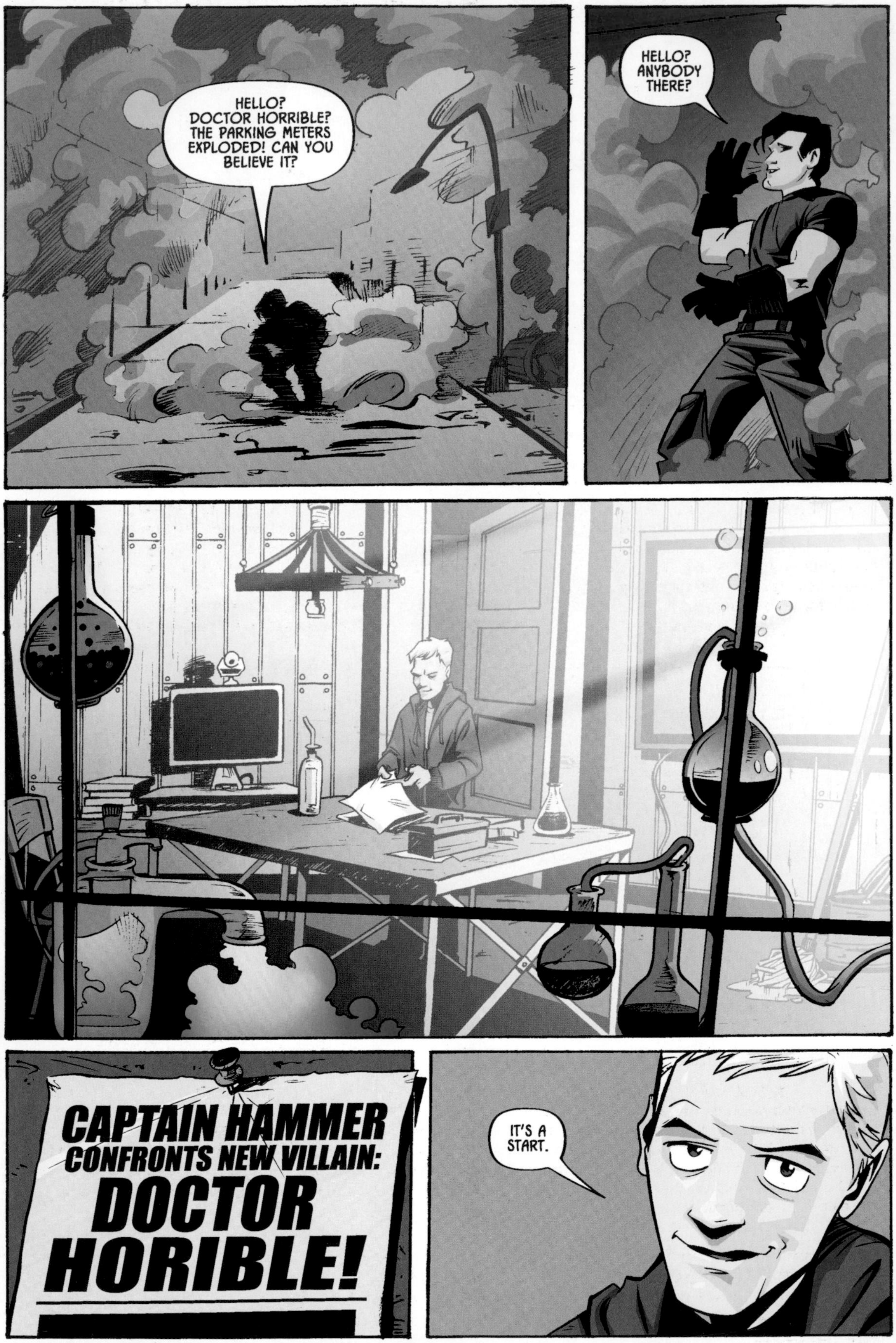

HELLO? DOCTOR HORRIBLE? THE PARKING METERS EXPLODED! CAN YOU BELIEVE IT?
HELLO? ANYBODY THERE?
CAPTAIN HAMMER CONFRONTS NEW VILLAIN: DOCTOR HORIBLE!
IT'S A START.

ALSO FROM DARK HORSE BOOKS

JOSS WHEDON GEORGES JEANTY
Buffy the vampire slayer
THE LONG WAY HOME

BUFFY THE VAMPIRE SLAYER SEASON EIGHT VOL. 1
Joss Whedon and Georges Jeanty
The smash-hit TV series continues, only in comics! Since the destruction of the Hellmouth, the slayers—newly legion—have gotten organized and are kicking some serious undead butt. But not everything's fun and firearms . . .
ISBN 978-1-59307-822-5 | $15.99

SERENITY
THE SHEPHERD'S TALE
JOSS WHEDON ZACK WHEDON CHRIS SAMNEE

SERENITY: THE SHEPHERD'S TALE
Zack Whedon and Chris Samnee
Who was Shepherd Book before meeting the Serenity crew, how did he become a trusted ally, and how did he find God in a bowl of soup? Answers to these and more questions are uncovered in this original graphic novel.
ISBN 978-1-59582-561-2 | $14.99

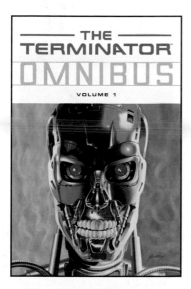

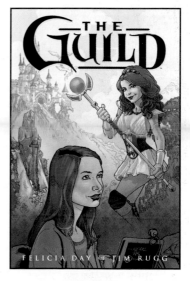

THE TERMINATOR
OMNIBUS
VOLUME 1

THE TERMINATOR OMNIBUS VOL. 1
Written by James Robinson, John Arcudi, Ian Edginton
Art by Chris Warner, Matt Wagner, Guy Davis, and others
Dark Horse brings in some of comics' top talent for this expansion of the Terminator mythos. *The Terminator Omnibus* Vol. 1 features over three hundred story pages in a full color, value-priced edition.
ISBN 978-1-59307-916-1 | $24.99

THE GUILD
FELICIA DAY & JIM RUGG

THE GUILD
Felicia Day and Jim Rugg
From the creator and star of the cult web series comes this prequel story, chronicling Cyd Sherman's life before joining the guild and revealing the origins of the Knights of Good.
ISBN 978-1-59582-549-0 | $ 12.99

AVAILABLE AT YOUR LOCAL COMICS SHOP OR BOOKSTORE! • To find a comics shop in your area, call 1-888-266-4226.
For more information or to order direct, visit darkhorse.com or call 1-800-862-0052 Mon.–Fri. 9 AM to 5 PM Pacific Time.

DARK HORSE BOOKS®
darkhorse.com

ALSO FROM DARK HORSE BOOKS

#1 NEW YORK TIMES BEST-SELLING AUTHOR
JANET EVANOVICH
ALEX EVANOVICH
ART BY JOËLLE JONES
TROUBLE MAKER
BOOK ONE A BARNABY AND HOOKER GRAPHIC NOVEL

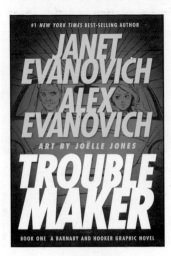

TROUBLEMAKER
BOOK ONE
Written by Janet Evanovich and Alex Evanovich
Art by Joëlle Jones

Janet Evanovich continues her *New York Times* best-selling Barnaby series with her very first graphic novel! Alex Barnaby, an auto mechanic and spotter for racecar driver Sam Hooker, is drawn to trouble like a palmetto bug to a day-old taco. Unfortunately, she's also drawn to Sam in the same way. There's no steering clear of trouble or Hooker when her friend Felicia calls for help.

ISBN 978-1-59582-488-2 | $17.99

BEASTS of BURDEN
ANIMAL RITES
EVAN DORKIN JILL THOMPSON

BEASTS OF BURDEN
VOLUME 1: ANIMAL RITES
Written by Evan Dorkin
Art by Jill Thompson

Welcome to Burden Hill–a picturesque little town adorned with white picket fences and green, green grass. Beneath this shiny exterior, Burden Hill harbors dark and sinister secrets, and it's up to a heroic gang of dogs–and one cat–to protect the town from the evil forces at work.

ISBN 978-1-59582-513-1 | $19.99

VOLUME 2: WEATHERED STATUES

THE END LEAGUE
VOLUME 2: WEATHERED STATUES
Written by Rick Remender
Art by Eric Canete

Writer Rick Remender continues his acclaimed new series joined by fan-favorite artist Eric Canete (*Iron Man*) for an all-new storyline. After the shocking events of the previous volume, Black and Arachnakid risk everything to take their revenge on the Smiling Man in his twisted city of Lore.

ISBN 978-1-59582-300-7 | $16.99

pop gun war

POP GUN WAR
Written and illustrated by Farel Dalrymple

Following a cast of disarmingly surreal characters—including a dwarf who becomes a giant and a young boy with wings growing from his shoulders, *Pop Gun War* is unlike anything you've ever seen. This handsome trade collects the first five issues of Dalrymple's daring and beautiful series.

ISBN 978-1-56971-934-3 | $13.99

AVAILABLE AT YOUR LOCAL COMICS SHOP OR BOOKSTORE! • To find a comics shop in your area, call 1-888-266-4226.
For more information or to order direct, visit darkhorse.com or call 1-800-862-0052 Mon.–Fri. 9 AM to 5 PM Pacific Time.

DARK HORSE BOOKS®
darkhorse.com